AMONG THE ENEMY

ALSO BY MARGARET PETERSON HADDIX

THE MISSING SERIES
Book 1: *Found*
Book 2: *Sent*
Book 3: *Sabotaged*

THE SHADOW CHILDREN SERIES
Among the Hidden
Among the Impostors
Among the Betrayed
Among the Barons
Among the Brave
Among the Free

The Girl with 500 Middle Names
Because of Anya
Say What?
Dexter the Tough
Running Out of Time
The House on the Gulf
Double Identity
Don't You Dare Read This, Mrs. Dunphrey
Leaving Fishers
Just Ella
Turnabout
Takeoffs and Landings
Escape from Memory
Uprising
Palace of Mirrors

AMONG THE ENEMY

MARGARET PETERSON
HADDIX

Simon & Schuster Books for Young Readers
New York London Toronto Sydney

SIMON & SCHUSTER BOOKS FOR YOUNG READERS
An imprint of Simon & Schuster Children's Publishing Division
1230 Avenue of the Americas, New York, NY 10020
Copyright © 2005 by Margaret Peterson Haddix
All rights reserved, including the right of reproduction in whole or in part in any form.
SIMON & SCHUSTER BOOKS FOR YOUNG READERS and colophon are trademarks of Simon & Schuster, Inc.
Also available in a Simon & Schuster Books for Young Readers hardcover edition.
Designed by Greg Stadnyk
The text of this book was set in Elysium.
Manufactured in the United States of America
First Simon & Schuster Books for Young Readers paperback edition October 2006
20 19 18 17 16 15
The Library of Congress has cataloged the hardcover edition as follows:
Haddix, Margaret Peterson.
Among the enemy / Margaret Peterson Haddix.—1st ed.
p. cm.
"A shadow children book."
Summary: In a society that allows families to have only two children, third child Matthias joins the Population Police to infiltrate their system.
ISBN 978-0-689-85796-6 (hc.)
[1. Conduct of life—Fiction. 2. Science fiction.] I. Title.
PZ7.H1164Ale 2005
[Fic]—dc22   2004009645
ISBN 978-0-689-85797-3 (pbk.)
ISBN 978-1-439-10672-3 (eBook)
0515 OFF

For Will and Jenna

AMONG THE ENEMY

AMONG THE HIDDEN

CHAPTER ONE

Matthias was sound asleep when the Population Police arrived at Niedler School.

It was the middle of the night, and Matthias was curled up on his narrow cot beside Percy's, in a roomful of narrow cots. It still bothered the boys that Alia couldn't sleep nearby. The cots were the most comfortable beds they'd ever had, but both boys still found themselves jerking awake several times each night, reaching out to protect a little girl who wasn't there.

But no instinct, no premonition alerted them when the Population Police trucks rolled up the school driveway. Matthias and Percy slept through the ominous rumble of the engines, the impatient rapping on the school's front door, the trample of boots in the hall. And then dozens of flashlights were suddenly blazing in their room, and Population Police officers were yelling at them, "Up! Up! Your country demands your service!"

Matthias's life before Niedler School had sometimes

required instant alertness, even when awakening from deep sleep. So while the other boys in the room sat up groggily or moaned without opening their eyes—"Huh?" "Wha's happ'ning?"—only Matthias and Percy had the presence of mind to gather up their belongings, to stuff their feet into socks and shoes before the officers herded everyone out of the room.

"Think they're getting the girls, too?" Percy whispered as the press of bodies around them moved down the hall.

"Don't know," Matthias said miserably. He craned his neck, trying to see over the boys in front of him, but they were all too tall. Anyhow, a line of Population Police officers stood beyond them, blocking his view of the other wing of Niedler School.

To distract himself, Matthias crammed a moth-eaten sweater over his head and pulled it down over his pajama top. The sweater was easier to wear than to carry, and it provided some small protection against the chill of the hall. Until the past week, Niedler School had had what Matthias viewed as the greatest luxury ever: central heat. But something had happened a week ago, and now the vents no longer breathed heat, the light switches no longer worked, the bathroom faucets no longer delivered water of any kind. The few teachers who hadn't run away wouldn't or couldn't say what had changed.

"Want to escape?" Percy asked, so quietly that Matthias had to read his friend's lips rather than relying on his ears to register any sound.

"Not without Alia," Matthias whispered back.

The other students were wedged around him so tightly, and the Population Police officers were watching the boys so closely, that Matthias would have laughed at anyone else who suggested escape. But Matthias had no doubt that Percy had already worked out a plan, that he could have spirited himself and Matthias out of the crowd without leaving a trace.

The mass of bodies reached the school's dining hall, and the Population Police let the boys stream in.

"Sit!" the officers ordered, again and again. "Sit!"

They seemed to expect unquestioning obedience, single-minded focus on reaching each designated seat. But Matthias dared to turn his head and look around. He wasn't sure whether to be relieved or disappointed when he saw a group of students in nightgowns already sitting on the opposite side of the dining hall. The girls. His heart started to pound when he spotted one small blond head in particular.

"Alia's at the third table from the left," he whispered to Percy. "Facing this way."

"If we crawl under the tables—," Percy began. But it was too late.

All the boys were seated now, and the top Population Police official—the one who had the most decorations on his uniform, anyway—stepped up to the podium at the front of the room.

"Do you have any food?" he thundered.

Silence. No one dared to answer.

"Are you all mute?" the official raged. "Are you all a pack of imbeciles?"

Mumbles broke out in the crowd. "Uh, no, sir." "No, no, no." "No food, sir." Matthias wasn't sure if all the others lacked the courage to speak loudly or if, like him, they knew better than to draw attention to themselves. But enough students whispered that the message carried to the front of the room.

The Population Police official frowned.

"You," he said, pointing to a timid, frail boy near the podium. "Stand up."

Trembling, the boy rose.

"When was the last time you ate?" the official asked.

"Yesterday?" the boy said. "The day before?"

"You don't know?" the Population Police official asked.

"No, sir. I mean, yes, sir. I mean, I don't know what you count as eating. It's been just broth since—since . . . last week?"

The Population Police official frowned. His eyes narrowed too, like he was mad that the boy was hungry.

"And what have you done to deserve food?" the official thundered.

The boy cowered, as if fearing that the man's voice alone could knock him over.

"Uh, I'm sorry, sir. I don't know, sir. I just—"

"You have done nothing!" The man's voice was even louder now. No matter how much he wanted to avoid being noticed, Matthias couldn't help flinching. Every child in the room did. Only the Population Police officers stood impassive.

The man raged on.

"You don't deserve to eat! You are a drain on your country's resources!"

The boy seemed to grow smaller and smaller, hunching down to avoid the man's wrath. The man seemed about to hit him but suddenly drew back.

"And yet," he said, his voice turning soft and cunning, "your country has a new leader. A wise, compassionate leader, willing to give you a chance to make up for your uselessness. Would you like that, young man?"

A new leader? Matthias thought. *How could that be?* His country had had the same leader for as long as he could remember. Baffled, he watched the boy's eager nodding.

"You will work for your Government," the man said soothingly, "and then you will deserve food. Then you will eat." As a final touch, he laid his hand gently on the boy's head, like he was giving him a blessing. Then the man looked out at the whole crowd of students.

"*All* of you will work," he said. "All of you will eat."

As if on cue, the other Population Police officers began urging the students to their feet, began hurrying them out another door. By working their way diagonally through the crowd, Matthias and Percy were just a few kids behind Alia as they stepped outdoors. But just as they reached her side, a Population Police officer lifted her onto the back of a truck. Turning, the officer muttered, "The little ones won't last a week in the work camp. Why are we bothering?"

"Orders," the man beside him grunted.

Percy and Matthias scrambled up behind Alia, just in time to see another officer sliding a thick fabric strip across her chest and lap.

"You're tying her down?" Matthias asked incredulously.

"It's a seat belt," the officer said. "I'm keeping her safe."

But Matthias heard the clink of the metal latch at the end of the fabric. He saw the officer turn a key before straightening up. Alia wasn't just tied down—she was locked into place.

"You're next," the officer said. "Sit down."

Matthias exchanged a quick glance with Percy, trying to hold an entire conversation with his eyes. *What are my other choices? . . . What do you think I should do?*

"I said, sit down!" the officer yelled, giving up all pretense of patience and kindness. He shoved Matthias to the floor of the truck, and Matthias's head hit the wooden wall that surrounded the truck bed. Then the officer slipped a seat belt across Matthias's body as well. Strangely, Matthias didn't hear the clink of the belt locking into place.

"You too," the officer screamed at Percy, shoving him down. "Hey, what's this? No personal possessions allowed."

He'd discovered the bundles of belongings Percy and Matthias had pulled together. He yanked them away and tossed them out the back of the truck, into the dark night.

"Won't we need clothes at the work camp?" Percy dared to ask.

"The Government will provide," the officer said. "The Government will provide everything you need."

Then the officer moved on to the next kid.

"You okay?" Percy whispered.

"I'll live," Matthias said, rubbing the knot that was already forming at the back of his head. "Alia?"

"I'm fine," the little girl said cheerfully. "What's our plan?"

"Cut the seat belts, then jump off the truck when no one's looking," Percy said.

"Sounds good to me," Matthias said.

He reached down into his pocket for his knife. But he'd forgotten: He was still wearing his pajama pants. His knife was in his other pants, in the bundle the Population Police officer had thrown off the truck.

"Percy?" he whispered, trying to keep the panic out of his voice, out of his mind. Surely Percy would have thought to keep his knife with him.

But even in the darkness, Matthias could recognize the look of dismay on Percy's face as Percy, too, shoved his hand down into an empty pocket.

"Alia?" Matthias asked. "Did you have time to bring any-thing with you when the Population Police came?"

Alia shook her head.

"I was asleep and somebody picked me up," she said.

"One of them." She pointed at the Population Police officer shoving kids down near the other side of the truck bed.

Alia's voice was calm, but Matthias thought it must have been terrifying for her to wake up in the arms of her worst enemy.

"So none of us has a knife," Percy muttered, with his usual ability to cut right to the point of a matter.

We're so stupid, Matthias thought. *Why weren't we sleeping with our clothes on under our pajamas? Why didn't we have all our tools stuffed in our pockets, all the time?* He knew the answer. They'd gone soft, living indoors. They'd started to believe they belonged in central heat, with electricity and hot and cold running water. They'd started to trust in their own safety.

It's all my fault, Matthias thought. He was the oldest. If he'd told the other two to stay on constant alert, they would have.

Angrily, he yanked on the belt holding him in place, straining against the trap he'd been caught in. Amazingly, the belt pulled clean away from the wall.

He was free.

Matthias stared at the unattached metal end of the belt in disbelief. He held it up into the dim light, just inches from his eyes, trying to puzzle out how it'd come apart.

"Matty!" Percy exploded in a low voice. He shoved Matthias's hand down. "Don't let *them* see."

Matthias hid the metal end of the belt back against the wooden wall. He was thinking again.

"Pull on your belts," he hissed to Percy and Alia. "Maybe they'll come loose too."

But no matter how much Percy and Alia strained and tugged and pulled, their belts stayed firmly locked in place.

The Population Police officers were done loading children onto the truck now. Several children were crying, but no harsh male voices barked orders at them anymore. The sobs floated up toward the dark sky unmixed with any sound except the churning of the trucks' engines. All the officials, Matthias realized, had retreated back to the trucks' cabs.

They were about to drive away.

Percy and Alia seemed to grasp the situation at the same time Matthias did.

"Matt-Matt, *go*," Alia said, using the name she'd given him back when she was a baby, barely able to talk.

"Save yourself," Percy urged, his voice cracking. "You can't save us."

Matthias looked back and forth between his two closest friends. No—"friends" was much too shallow a word to describe his relationship with Percy and Alia. They were like a brother and a sister who, by some strange accident, happened not to have the same parents. They were as much a part of him as his own arms; he couldn't imagine living without them.

"No," he said. "We stick together. Always."

He slid back against the wooden wall and tucked the

broken end of his belt behind his back, hiding his chance at freedom.

Then the truck lurched forward, and it was too late to change his mind.

CHAPTER TWO

The wind whipped Matthias's hair into his face as the truck picked up speed. It would be easiest to close his eyes and lean back and let whatever was going to happen, happen. But he could feel Alia shivering beside him; he could feel the scrawny muscles in Percy's arm tensed with fear.

"Maybe it won't be so bad, where we're going," Matthias said.

"Maybe we can still escape," Percy whispered back. "Like last time."

They'd been picked up by the Population Police once before. Matthias still had nightmares about that awful time in their lives. Samuel, the kindly man who'd raised them, had been killed, and Matthias was suddenly in charge, even though he'd been only ten years old (give or take—none of them knew how old they really were). For weeks, Matthias had lived in fear that he would fail the other two, that they would starve or be hurt or killed. Or captured. He could still feel the hand of the Population Police officer on his shoulder, still hear the echo of the booming voice shouting out, "You're under arrest! Those I.D.'s are fake!"

But in Population Police prison, only moments before Matthias and Percy and Alia thought they were going to be executed, a man had come to them and whispered, "I'm on your side. . . ."

It was tempting to dwell on that moment, to hope for another miracle. But Matthias's memory backed up a little. He frowned at Percy.

"This isn't like the last time," he said slowly. "They aren't arresting us. They didn't even ask to see our I.D.'s."

As far as he knew, Matthias had never had a valid I.D. He didn't know his real name. He didn't even know if he'd been given a name before his parents, whoever they were, had abandoned him. Samuel had always told him and Percy and Alia that they were the lucky ones. They were lucky they'd been abandoned, not killed.

"There are laws in this land," Samuel had told them. "Evil laws. A woman who's had two children isn't allowed to have any more. That's why babies show up on my doorstep. . . ."

Samuel's doorstep had been a concrete block in a dark alley. His home had been an abandoned tunnel that flooded every spring and was cold and dank year-round. But Samuel had never turned away a child, even when hiding children put his own life in danger. He'd taken them in and taught them everything he knew: how to survive on the streets; how to work for good in an evil world; how to make fake identity cards for other illegal children.

What if the Population Police no longer cared about identity cards? What if they'd figured out some other way to decide whether people had the right to live?

"That man in the dining hall said there's a new leader," Matthias said now, trying to puzzle everything out.

"Yeah, a new leader who thinks little kids don't deserve to eat," Percy snorted. "We've *got* to escape. Don't we have anything sharp at all?"

Hopelessly, the three of them felt around them, as if they really thought a spare knife would be lying on the floor of the truck bed. Matthias, sliding his hand along the rough wood, found only a gaping hole where the floor was broken off. Daringly, he reached down through the hole, pulling back only when he felt the breeze from the spinning tires directly below. Now it was his turn to shiver. What if Alia had fallen through this hole? What if, even now, she slid forward and dropped through it, regardless of the seat belt?

"Alia, sit back," he commanded roughly. "It's not safe over here."

"Did you get a splinter?" Alia asked.

Sometimes it was hard to remember that Alia was only six or seven, only a little kid. She'd withstood life on the streets and Population Police interrogation. But when Matthias warned her about danger, she still thought about splinters before imminent death.

"No, I'm fine," Matthias insisted, even though his mind was supplying a horrid picture of what might have happened if he'd reached his arm down only a little farther, if the tires had caught it and sucked his body down and he'd been crushed beneath the wheels.

Did Percy and Alia worry about the worst possibilities as much as he did?

Hoping to clear his mind, Matthias stood halfway up, his hands searching higher and higher on the wooden wall behind him. He thought it was still dark enough that none of the Population Police would see him. He looked out over the truckload of huddled children, most of them too exhausted and terrified even to whimper now. Through the cracks in the wood, he could see the lights of the other trucks. How many? Four, five, six? All carrying dozens of children—where? And why?

"The little ones won't last a week in the work camp," the one Population Police officer had said.

Matthias's search became even more frantic. He dared to reach higher. He was rewarded with a sudden pain in his hand.

"Ow," he moaned, and pulled his hand back to rub the new wound, which was already bleeding.

"What is it?" Percy asked.

"There's a nail sticking out. I cut my hand," Matthias said.

A nail . . .

Matthias forgot his pain and reached up again, a little

more cautiously. The point of the nail was facing him, so he had to put his hand out through the crack and work the nail out from the other side. He was scared it was stuck in the wood too tightly, scared he'd drop it even if he managed to pull it out. But a few seconds later, he crouched down holding the rusty, bent nail like a great treasure. It *was* a great treasure. A gift.

Thank you, God, he whispered silently, an old habit he'd learned from Samuel. The old man had believed everything good was a gift, and Matthias could remember him giving prayers of thanks for lukewarm cups of tea, wilted sprigs of flowers, even floods when they didn't reach the heights of previous years.

"Got it?" Percy asked. "Help Alia first."

Matthias turned and began sawing away at Alia's seat belt with the point of the nail. His muscles began to ache before he'd cut through even two or three threads, but he kept trying.

"Get some sleep," he told Percy and Alia. "This is going to take a while."

Obediently, the other two hunched over and seemed to slip instantly into unconsciousness. As far as Matthias could tell, all the other children were asleep now too. He felt alone, just him and his rusty nail moving back and forth, back and forth.

Matthias couldn't have said how many hours it took him to completely sever the seat belt holding Alia in place. But when he was done, he rewarded himself by rising to his knees, stretching his cramped muscles. Through the crack in the wooden wall, he could see the first glimmers of dawn on the horizon.

"Not much time left," he muttered to himself. He clutched the nail again and began attacking Percy's seat belt with renewed vigor. The three of them would need the cover of darkness if they planned to jump off the back of the truck. Matthias had a picture in his mind of exactly how their escape should go: As soon as they were all free of the seat belts, they'd move to the very back of the truck. None of the children they stepped over would wake up. Then, when the truck slowed down going around a curve—or, better yet, came to a stop at a road sign—Alia, Percy, and Matthias would roll off into the shadows. Easy as breathing, as Samuel used to say.

Tears stung at Matthias's eyes, but he wouldn't have been able to say whether they were from missing Samuel or from exhaustion and fear—fear that they'd reach the work camp before he cut through Percy's seat belt, fear that the sun would come up too soon, fear that he'd fail Percy and Alia once again. Frantically, he brushed the tears away and went back to scraping the nail against the fabric. Harder, faster, harder, faster . . .

Percy woke up.

"What's wrong?" he asked, as calm as ever.

"Sun's coming up, and this stupid nail—I think I could chew the belt off faster," Matthias muttered.

"Let me try," Percy said.

Matthias handed over the nail, though his hand was too stiff to unclench completely.

Percy began sliding the nail against the belt in slow, deliberate slices. Matthias couldn't stand it. He peered out through the cracks in the wooden wall again. He couldn't gauge the position of the sun now because they were driving through what appeared to be a clump of trees. Then they rounded a curve into a brief clearing, and suddenly Matthias could see far down the road, into a valley ahead. What he saw terrified him even more than the rising sun.

"Percy!" he muttered urgently. "What's a work camp look like?"

Percy looked up.

"How am I supposed to know?" he asked.

"Lots of lights, high fences, guardhouses everywhere?" Matthias asked.

"Sounds more like a prison, but—yeah, maybe," Percy replied.

"Then we're almost there!" Matthias hissed.

Percy's answer was to bend back over the nail, pressing down harder but moving no faster.

"Percy, that's no good. There's no time."

Percy didn't answer right away. Matthias had to bend in low to hear him say, "Take Alia, then. You two escape. Forget me."

"No," Matthias moaned.

The truck slowed down, navigating another curve. *A missed opportunity*, Matthias thought. The truck was virtually at a standstill. But he couldn't leave Percy behind. He couldn't. In a panic, he grabbed the nail from Percy's hand.

"What—?" Percy started to ask.

There wasn't time to explain. Matthias crawled away from Percy and plunged his arm down through the hole in the floor, plunged the nail into the slow-moving tire below.

At first nothing happened, and Matthias had time to agonize: How could he have been so stupid and impulsive? How could he have thrown away the nail, Percy's only chance?

Then, as the truck sped up again, there was a noise like a gunshot below them. Matthias had been hoping for just a flat tire, a slow leak that would buy them extra time. But the tire had blown out instead, bursting into shreds beneath them. The truck tilted crazily and veered off the road, as if the driver was struggling to regain control.

"Hold on!" Matthias yelled.

The truck crashed into the trees lining the road and came to a sudden stop in an explosion of breaking glass and smashing steel. It sounded like the truck had hit a wall. It sounded like the end of the world.

Then Matthias looked up and saw a huge tree falling straight toward them.

CHAPTER *THREE*

The tree hit with an earth-shattering thud. The entire truck seemed to shudder to pieces. An avalanche of leaves and twigs rained down on Matthias, but miraculously, he felt no large branches strike his body.

"Percy?" he whispered into the darkness.

"I'm here," Percy whispered back. "Look."

It was a useless command. The enormous tree that now covered them blocked out all light. But Matthias reached out in the direction of Percy's voice, and he felt what Percy was holding out to him: It was the metal clasp of Percy's seat belt, surrounded by jagged wood. The falling tree had shattered the wood wall. Percy was free now too.

"Thank God," Matthias murmured. "Let's get Alia and go. Alia?"

No answer.

"Alia?" Matthias said louder, and reached out to the other side, to where Alia had been sitting. His fingers dug through leaves, more leaves, and prickly twigs. And then a branch too large to shove aside.

Cold fear seemed to crawl along every nerve in his body. He reached under the branch, brushing the floor of the truck bed. The floor seemed to be covered with some sort of sticky liquid now.

Dew, he tried to tell himself. *Dew or sap. Tree sap is sticky, isn't it?*

But he knew what the liquid really was. Blood.

"Alia?" he cried again, his voice coming out in a hoarse gasp.

Someone moaned on the other side of the branch.

Matthias dived over the branch. Mercifully, Alia was right there. He scooped her up into his arms.

"We've got to go, Alia," he muttered. *"Now."*

Her head flopped loosely against his shoulder.

She's breathing, Matthias told himself. *I know she is. I heard her moan. She* must *still be alive.* He took the time to wrap his hand around her wrist. Her pulse beat against his fingers. Faintly.

"Come on, Percy," Matthias commanded, panic making his voice raspy. "I found Alia. Follow me."

Percy put one hand on Matthias's shoulder, and the two of them fought their way through the branches. Sometimes they had to shove other children out of their way too. Sometimes the children moaned or complained: "Ouch! You stepped on my fingers!" Some of the children were crying or screaming: "Help me! Help me!" "My leg!"

MARGARET PETERSON HADDIX

"My arm!" "I'm trapped!" The voices wove together into one roaring tide of pain and fear, until Matthias could no longer make out the individual words.

Some of the children were silent. Somehow that was worse.

Matthias tried not to think about what that meant. He focused on moving forward, lifting Alia over the branches, protecting her from the twigs that threatened to snag her nightgown and scratch her skin. He ignored his aching muscles, his straining back, anything that might distract him from his escape.

Finally he reached the back edge of the truck bed.

"You go first. I'll hand Alia down to you," he whispered over his shoulder to Percy.

Percy slipped past Matthias, shimmying down to the ground. Stiffly, Matthias knelt down and lowered Alia into Percy's arms. Alia was all skin and bones, a wisp of a child, but Percy still staggered under her weight. Matthias jumped down, and Percy handed Alia back to him.

"Into the woods?" Percy asked.

Matthias didn't have enough energy to answer, but it didn't matter. He and Percy were already stumbling into the underbrush. Matthias was so exhausted that his legs seemed to be moving of their own will. Branches lashed against his face, but he barely noticed. As long as they didn't hurt Alia, he didn't care.

"Matthias?" Percy said after some time had passed.

"Matthias? I don't think anyone followed us. We're safe now. We can stop and rest."

Matthias sank to his knees, still cradling Alia's body against his chest. The woods around him were light now; the sun had risen fully while Matthias wasn't looking, wasn't thinking, wasn't conscious of anything except the need to hold on to Alia and move forward. Only now did he finally dare to look down at Alia's face.

She had an open wound at her right temple, and blood matted in her hair. Her skin was so pale, it frightened him.

"Why won't she wake up?" he asked Percy. "What if—?" He forced the words out. "What if she dies?"

"She won't," Percy said fiercely. "We'll find someone to help."

Matthias began struggling to get back on his feet, but his legs felt useless now, his arms could no longer lift Alia.

"Stop it," Percy said. "You're too tired. You'll drop her, and that will be worse. Get some sleep and we'll walk more later. I'll watch over Alia."

Matthias wanted to protest, to tell Percy, *No, let's keep going.* But his eyes were already closing, his mind already slipping into a nightmare.

If Alia dies, he thought, with his last burst of consciousness, *it will be my fault.*

CHAPTER *FOUR*

When Matthias woke up, hours later, Percy was crouched beside him, staring off into space. Matthias would have expected Percy to say, *Good morning,* or *Feeling better?* or, best of all, *Alia's going to be all right.*

Instead, Percy blinked once and said in a flat voice, "Samuel would have stopped and helped those other kids."

Matthias felt as though Percy had stabbed him right through the heart. Of course Samuel would have helped the other kids injured by the falling tree—the kids injured because of Matthias plunging the nail into the tire. Even if it meant getting caught himself, Samuel would have tended their wounds, stroked their brows, comforted them. Even if they were going to die anyway, he would have stayed by their side until the very end.

Oh, dear Lord, Matthias prayed. *Did some of those kids die because of me?*

"We could go back," he said without much hope.

Percy shook his head.

"There were other trucks, remember? I'm sure the other drivers came back. It's too late now."

Matthias winced. Those words hurt too. *Too late, too late . . .* He'd made a decision in a split second, when he wasn't thinking of anyone but himself and Percy and Alia. His aching hand clenched, like he was still holding the nail, still had a chance to make a different decision. A decision that wouldn't leave any innocent children dead.

But it was too late.

"And Alia?" he whispered. "Is she—?"

"She's still sleeping," Percy said, pointing.

Matthias raised himself on one elbow so he could see the little girl, lying flat on her back on a bed of leaves nearby.

"She's unconscious," he corrected Percy.

"Same thing," Percy said.

"No." Matthias shook his head. Why didn't Percy understand? Sleep was what healthy children did when they were tired. Unconscious was someone sick, someone on the verge of death.

"I washed her wounds," Percy said. "I tore off a piece of her nightgown for a bandage for her head. I made sure it was a clean part of the nightgown."

Like that's going to matter, Matthias thought.

Percy was looking at Matthias strangely.

"I don't think any of the Population Police saw us escape," Percy said. "No one followed us. I found a stream with clear water and a tree that had all sorts of nuts underneath it. It wasn't hard to get them open with a rock. So we have food."

Matthias knew what Percy was doing. This was a game that Samuel had taught them. When times were bad, they always recited all the good things they could think of. Matthias was supposed to add to the list, then finish with, *And God loves us.* But the only good thing that Matthias could think of was, *Alia's not dead yet.* And that was a blessing with a curse hidden inside it. "Not dead yet" just meant that the full weight of Matthias's pain and grief was lurking a little ways ahead.

He stood up abruptly.

"We should start walking," he said. "We've wasted too much time already."

"All right," Percy said. "Where do you think we should go?"

But Matthias hadn't thought about a destination. He just wanted to move, to get away.

Percy had everything figured out anyway.

"I thought about it while you and Alia were sleeping," he said. "I think we should go to Mr. Hendricks. He's got that separate cottage—even if the Population Police raided his school when they raided Niedler, maybe they didn't catch him."

Mr. Hendricks was the headmaster of a school that Percy, Matthias, and Alia had visited, but not attended, before they went to Niedler. And Mr. Hendricks was friends with Mr. Talbot, the man who'd saved them the first time they'd been captured by the Population Police. He'd been with them at Hendricks School too. Matthias remembered their time with Mr. Hendricks as a joyous vacation. It'd been the first time he'd felt truly happy after Samuel's death.

That was before I became a murderer, he thought.

"Well?" Percy asked, and Matthias had to squint at him, trying to remember what they'd been talking about. "Should we go to Mr. Hendricks, or do you have a better plan?"

Matthias shrugged. "That's fine," he said.

He bent over and picked up Alia, and the strain on his muscles felt good. He deserved the pain in his arms, the ache in his back. He deserved worse.

Behind him, he heard Percy mumble an end to the List of Good Things game: "We're alive. We're together. And God loves us."

Matthias started walking as quickly as he could so Percy wouldn't see the tears streaming down his face.

CHAPTER *FIVE*

ater Matthias would remember very little about that
day of walking. He and Percy were city boys used to
darting through crowds, navigating by the cracks in the
pavement, surviving on other people's garbage. But they'd
once had to spend several days in a wilderness, and that
experience was evidently enough to help them move eas-
ily through this woods. Matthias sidestepped the poison
ivy without even thinking about it; he ducked under low-
hanging branches without breaking his stride.

That, at least, was good, because his mind was elsewhere.

Don't think about the truck, he kept telling himself. *Don't
think about the other children. You are rescuing Alia. You are taking her to safety.*

His arms went numb from carrying her, but he refused
to take breaks, he refused to let Percy try to carry her. He
wasn't sure exactly how far it would be to Mr. Hendricks's
house, but he didn't intend to stop until he got there.

Percy had other ideas. As dusk fell over the woods, Percy asked, "Are you looking for shelter for the night yet?"

"Shelter?" Matthias repeated stupidly.

"If we can't find a hut or a shed, a cave would do. We've got to find someplace before it's too dark for walking."

Matthias's brain seemed to have gone as numb as his arms. He'd forgotten about darkness, forgotten they had no candles or lamps or flashlights. But he didn't like Percy's notion of huts or sheds, places where people would be—people who might turn them in to the Population Police.

"We slept outside before. With Nina," Matthias said. Nina was a friend of theirs who'd been with them during their other outdoors experience, when they'd been escaping from a Population Police prison. In the beginning, Matthias hadn't known whether or not he could trust Nina. He hadn't known if she was good or bad.

Am I good or bad? Now that I've done something awful too. . . .

He flinched, as if he could physically move away from that question. He forced himself to focus on what Percy was saying.

"—was summertime before. It was warm enough to sleep outside then. Remember how Nina complained about the heat? It's November now, and it's been getting colder all day long. . . . I don't know, but it almost feels like it might snow tonight. And Alia's just wearing that nightgown. . . ."

Matthias hugged Alia even closer. He should have taken

his sweater off and put it on Alia hours ago. Why hadn't he thought of that? Why hadn't Percy suggested it?

"Let's go out closer to the road and see if there are any houses," Percy finished.

All day long they'd been walking parallel to a paved road. It was their guide for getting to Mr. Hendricks. But they'd wanted to stay far enough away that they wouldn't be spotted from any car windows.

Strangely, now that he thought about it, Matthias couldn't remember hearing a single car or truck go by.

Percy was already tramping off toward the road. Matthias wanted to call him back, to try to come up with a better plan. But Percy disappeared behind a tree before Matthias could put his thoughts together. Matthias struggled to follow the younger boy. In this section of the woods, the road lay downhill, and Matthias was terrified of falling with Alia in his arms.

The ground was wet, and his feet slipped out from under him. He landed hard on his rear.

"Oohh," Alia moaned.

"I'm sorry. I'm so sorry," Matthias muttered.

He didn't think she could hear him, but her eyelids fluttered—once, twice . . . Then, amazingly, they opened all the way.

"You're awake?" Matthias whispered, not quite able to believe it.

"Hurts," she mumbled.

"I know, I know. I didn't mean to fall down. Percy's off

finding us a place for the night. Everything's okay, now that you're awake." Matthias beamed at her.

Alia squinted up at him. She blinked as if the dim light of dusk was blinding and painful.

"I think . . . I think I was awake before," she whispered. "You . . . were . . . carrying me?"

"Yes," Matthias said. "We're taking you to help, because of the tree falling on you."

Alia winced and her eyelids closed again.

"Don't remember . . . any . . . tree," she murmured. "Don't remember . . . Why aren't we at school?"

It scared Matthias that she didn't seem to remember the Population Police taking them away. It scared him the way her head sagged against his arm again.

"Percy?" he called softly, wanting the other boy there for reassurance, for comfort.

"Over here," Percy answered from far down the hillside. "I think—"

But Matthias couldn't hear what Percy thought. Because that was when the first gunshot rang out.

CHAPTER *SIX*

Matthias reacted instinctively, somersaulting himself and Alia down the hill until they came to rest behind a huge log. Protection. Alia screamed with the pain of being moved so roughly, but even Matthias could barely hear her over the sudden barrage of gunfire.

It took Matthias a few minutes to realize that no one was shooting at him and Alia, that all the bullets were whizzing and zinging farther down the hill.

"Percy," he breathed out, in a way that might have been a prayer.

He dared to raise his head to peer over the log. From this vantage point, he could see a cabin's roof and a swath of empty road. At first it seemed that the gunfire was coming out of nowhere—phantom guns firing phantom bullets, maybe. But then he saw a rustle of movement on the opposite side of the road. In the uncertain light of dusk, he could make out men in dark uniforms. Population Police uniforms.

They sent that many men after us, with guns? For three unarmed children? he wondered.

But—he squirmed around to get a better view—the Population Police weren't aiming their guns even in the direction where Percy had been standing. They were shooting at the cabin.

And someone inside was shooting back at them.

Not Percy, Matthias told himself. When the gunfire had started, Percy's voice had come from a closer spot than the cabin. And, as far as Matthias knew, Percy had never touched a gun in his life. Even if he'd found a gun in the cabin, Percy wouldn't have picked it up and started shooting.

Oh, please, let that not be Percy, Matthias prayed. He could tell: Whoever was in the cabin didn't have a chance against the Population Police.

He was so desperate to find Percy that he raised his head even higher, so he could scan the entire hillside. In the failing light, everything was in shadows, but if Matthias peered hard enough, maybe—

The sound of gunfire stopped suddenly. Matthias froze, his ears still ringing. Down below, the Population Police officers swarmed across the road, surrounding the cabin. Matthias ducked his head down behind the log again, but he kept peeking out. He heard a splintering sound that probably meant the officers had kicked in the cabin door. Then they began dragging out dead bodies. One, two, three, four, five. . . . How many people had been crowded into that small cabin? The bodies kept coming. Matthias couldn't see all of them, but as far as he could tell, none of them was Percy.

Matthias's ears were recovering a little, enough that he could catch snatches of the Population Police officials' conversation.

"Seventeen rebels, just as our informant said," a harsh voice said.

"Fools."

Matthias could see the man who said that. He seemed to be leaning over one of the bodies, the way someone might lean over and kiss a child's forehead.

This man spat on the dead body instead.

"What do we do with them now?" somebody asked. "Carry them back with us?"

"Are you kidding? Don't you remember how far we had to hike to get here? I'm not carrying any corpse five miles in the dark."

"What's wrong? Scared of ghosts?" someone teased.

"Scared of getting blood on my uniform. Tell me again why we didn't just drive here?"

"The element of surprise was necessary," a steely voice said. It must have belonged to the group's leader, because everyone else fell silent. "Here's what we do. Take their I.D. cards, then pile these bodies by the side of the road. Then somebody—you, Sanders—make a sign. We want everyone who comes by here to see what happens to rebels."

"What should the sign say?" a timid voice asked. "'They was rebels'?"

"No, no," the leader said impatiently. "We don't want anyone thinking it's possible to rebel."

"But—"

"The sign will say, 'Enemies of the People.' Now do it!"

"Yes, sir!"

The officers scurried to obey.

Matthias watched with a growing sense of fear. He could see where they were piling the bodies, and any second he expected to see Percy's striped flannel pajama pants, or his black shoes with the hole in only one sole. Percy had been so proud of those shoes, the best he'd ever owned in all his life.

Without realizing it, Matthias had been counting each thud of every dead body landing on the pile. At the same time that he reached seventeen, the Population Police officers stepped back, as though their work was done.

Matthias had seen no striped pajamas, no holey shoes. But it was nearly dark—how could he be sure?

"Do you think he'll let us go now?" someone whined.

"Sir, should we search the rest of the area?" another man asked.

Matthias held his breath.

"No," the leader decided. "We did what we came to do. We could spend our whole lives looking through this wasteland, and for what? Back to headquarters! Now!"

The Population Police officers melted back into the woods on the other side of the road, as silently as if they were shadows themselves.

"Matt-Matt," Alia murmured.

"Shh," Matthias said. "Wait."

It was too dark now to see Alia's face; he couldn't be sure if she was awake or not. He couldn't be sure what she'd heard or what she understood. He waited long, agonizing minutes, in case the Population Police came back. Then he whistled a soft imitation of a whip-poor-will. He and Percy had used that as a signal many times before.

Poor-will! Poor-will! echoed below him. Except it wasn't an echo. It was Percy.

Matthias felt like screaming for joy, rushing down the hill immediately. But he stopped himself. He picked up Alia again and inched through the darkness. He had to call and wait for Percy's answer again and again. Each call and response unnerved him. Percy should have been moving toward Matthias as Matthias moved toward him, so they could meet halfway. But Percy's *Poor-will! Poor-will!* stayed in one spot.

Finally, after what felt like hours of stumbling through near-total darkness, Matthias thought he was close enough to whisper.

"Percy?"

A hand grabbed Matthias's ankle. Matthias crouched awkwardly, almost thrown off balance by the weight of Alia's body. He felt around on the ground. Dead leaves, furry moss, Percy's bloody leg . . .

Bloody?

"Percy!" Matthias hissed, fear overriding caution. "What happened to you?"

"Bullet," Percy said. It sounded like he was talking through clenched teeth. "Shot."

And then Matthias felt Percy's head loll over to the side, against Matthias's shoe.

Percy had passed out.

CHAPTER SEVEN

A s well as he could, Matthias tried raising Percy's head up again. But it was impossible to balance Alia on his lap and lift Percy at the same time.

"Percy, *no*, I need you," he argued.

He remembered how Samuel had always said, "God will never give you more than you can bear." But how could Matthias bear this? Both Percy and Alia injured and in such great pain and maybe dying . . .

"Oh, God, no," Matthias whispered, or maybe he was crying. He reached out for Percy's leg again, as if he believed his plea would make the wound miraculously heal itself. But blood was still seeping out along the gash in Percy's pajama pants. Lots of blood. Percy whimpered and jerked away from Matthias's hand.

Shouldn't touch, germs, infection, Matthias thought in a jumbled way. He was too horrified to think clearly, but the words "soap and water" fought their way into his mind.

I'm in the wilderness! Where am I supposed to find soap and water? he wanted to shout. But then the answer came to him.

The cabin.

If Matthias had stopped to consider how hard it would be to get both Alia and Percy down to the cabin, he might have given up right then. But the thought that kept cycling through his mind was, *Can't leave Alia, can't leave Percy, can't leave Alia, can't leave Percy. . . .* If he put Alia down to carry Percy, she might freeze to death before he could come back. If he left Percy behind and took Alia first, he might not be able to find Percy again in the dark. And then he'd have to wait for the morning light, and Percy could have bled to death by then.

What if Percy bled to death anyhow?

Don't think about that, he commanded himself.

He forced himself to concentrate on shifting Alia's limp body to one side, so he could support her with just one arm looped around her waist. With his other arm he reached down—awkwardly, almost toppling over—and wedged his hand under Percy's armpit. And then he began dragging both of them downhill.

He made slow, torturous progress, and both of them whimpered and moaned and cried out in their sleep, in pain. He was of two minds about their cries. At least they were still alive—but, oh, how could he be the one hurting them?

The trek down the hill took so long, Matthias was almost surprised when he lifted his head and saw a wall of logs directly in front of him. He had a moment of worrying that there might be Population Police guards remaining behind in the cabin—or perhaps more rebels left alive who might feel no friendlier toward Matthias than they did toward the Population Police. But he was too desperate to give that worry much thought.

"Just a—little—farther," he grunted to his two friends, even though they probably couldn't hear him.

He dragged them around to the front of the cabin and then lifted them, one by one, over the splintered door.

Inside the cabin was utter darkness.

Well, of course it is. What did I expect?

The last, lingering light of dusk illuminated only the first few inches inside the shattered doorway. Even as Matthias huddled there with Percy and Alia, that light seemed to fade and disappear.

We've survived in darkness before, Matthias reminded himself. For most of their time in Population Police prison, they'd been in an underground dungeon and had gone for days without seeing sunlight.

Percy and Alia weren't injured then, Matthias thought. *And we had candles that we could light in an emergency.*

Maybe there were candles in the cabin as well.

Even though every muscle in his body cried out in exhaustion, Matthias forced himself to reach out and grope around on the floor. He tried not to think about how many people had just died in the cabin.

"God rest their souls," he murmured, another Samuel

saying that somehow gave him the courage to keep reaching out, keep grasping for hope. All he asked for was a single candle and a single match, although a flashlight would be easier to work with. And he certainly wouldn't complain if he found medical supplies just lying around, waiting for him. . . .

At first he found only splinters. The floor was made of rough wooden planks that hadn't been sanded and didn't fit together well. The gaps between the planks were so wide that Matthias began to fear an entire book of matches could be hidden between two planks and Matthias would never know. So he fell into a pattern of sweeping his entire hand across a plank (carefully, trying to avoid the splinters), then wedging his fingers down between the cracks before moving on to the next plank.

That was how he discovered the secret latch.

Matthias didn't know what it was when his fingers brushed it, tucked away on the underside of one of the planks. But it was the first thing he'd touched that wasn't wood, and it puzzled him: Who would put a round, hard knob underneath a floor? He felt all around it, pushing it from side to side. When he pushed it to the right, something clicked.

And then the floor rose up before him.

CHAPTER *EIGHT*

Matthias was so stunned, it took him a few minutes even to wonder how he could see the floor moving.

There was a light. Under the floor.

He blinked a few times, and the sight before him began to make sense. He'd found the latch for a trapdoor, leading to an underground room.

Matthias slid over to the trapdoor opening—for it was actually just a small square that had moved, not the entire floor—and peered down. A ladder led down to a tidy room illuminated by one dim lantern. A row of cots stood at one end of the room, and he could just barely make out a sink at the other end.

Cots. A sink.

"I think I just found us a place to stay for the night," he said aloud to Percy and Alia. "And then you'll both be fine in the morning. Okay?"

His voice sounded strange and croaky in the dark night. Neither of his friends answered.

He pulled Alia toward him and began struggling to carry her down the ladder. He laid her as gently as he could on one of the cots and covered her with a blanket he found on the floor.

"I'll try to find some food for you as soon as I take care of Percy," he told her.

Her only response was a moan. The bandage Percy had fashioned for her had fallen off somewhere in the woods, so the wound on her head was exposed, all seepy and puffy-looking. A few strands of her hair were plastered to the wound, and Matthias felt faint at the thought of having to pull them away, hurting her even more.

"I'll be right back," he promised her.

He went back up the ladder. He tried carrying Percy down the same way he had Alia: over his shoulder. But Percy was nearly as tall and heavy as Matthias himself, and Matthias couldn't work out the proper arrangement of arms and legs. Halfway down the ladder, Matthias fell, and Percy landed right on top of him on the packed-dirt floor. Percy let out a roar of agony.

"I'm sorry. I'm sorry," Matthias apologized, but even the fall didn't awaken Percy.

Matthias struggled to his feet. Ignoring the pain in his own legs and spine, he dragged Percy over to a cot near Alia's. Percy left a trail of blood behind him.

How much blood can somebody lose and still live? Matthias wondered.

"I'll stop the bleeding now," he promised Percy. "Right

after I shut the trapdoor. When the trapdoor's shut, no one can find us down here. We're safe. I think there's some food down here—oh, yes! I see some bread over there on a shelf. I'll soak that in water and feed it to you and Alia. And I can tear up some of these blankets for bandages. . . ."

He wanted so badly for one of his friends to finish his list of blessings for him with *And God loves us.* Then he would be able to believe that the underground room *was* a safe place, that nobody would find them there, that his friends' wounds would heal. But his voice trailed off into silence, and no one answered him, no one at all.

CHAPTER NINE

Matthias did everything he could for his friends, but there was so much he didn't know. Could Percy's leg heal even if Matthias didn't take the bullet out? What did it mean that Alia flickered in and out of consciousness and seemed barely aware even when she was awake?

"They'll both be fine tomorrow," he told himself firmly. He managed to choke down a bit of bread and water himself, then blew out the lantern and curled up on a cot between his two friends.

He woke, hours later, to the sound of Alia crying. He lit the lantern and crouched by her cot.

"Shh," he murmured. "I'm here."

Alia stared up at him.

"Why doesn't it stop hurting?" she asked. "It feels like my head cracked in half, and every time I move, it cracks open some more." She flinched, as if just the act of talking was painful.

"Shh. Go back to sleep" was the best comfort Matthias

could offer. He wished he had some aspirin, but maybe even that wouldn't be enough for her.

He lay back down on his own cot, but sleep was impossible now.

What can I do, God? he prayed desperately. *How can I help Alia? How can I save Percy?*

He got up and took the lantern around the room, searching more thoroughly than he'd searched the night before. The cupboards and shelves over the sink contained an amazing quantity of food: bread and potatoes, apples, even a hunk of cheese. But that was all there was.

"Why did they even have this room?" he muttered to himself. It must have been hard work digging out this huge space. Why hadn't the cabin's owners just built a larger cabin?

Because they had something to hide. . . .

Matthias walked slowly around the room, stopping every few paces to tap his foot on the dirt floor. Then he felt carefully along the walls.

He found what he was looking for behind one of the cabinets over the sink. The wood wall swung away, revealing a safe with a combination lock.

Percy was the smart one, and Alia was the one with a sixth sense for picking locks. But neither of them could help Matthias now. At least he had determination on his side. He turned the numbered lock slowly, listening for clicks. A hope had begun to grow inside him. Maybe the seventeen "rebels" in the cabin had been smuggling medical supplies.

Sometimes people did that. Once, Matthias remembered, a man had come and asked Samuel if they could use his tunnel to store some stolen medicine.

"You'd be helping people, old man," the smuggler had said. "The people who are going to get this medicine would die without it. The Government certainly isn't doing anything for them."

Samuel had asked the man for a few days to think it over. Matthias remembered watching Samuel sit and pray and think. Finally he told the smuggler no.

"What about the people the medicine was intended for?" Samuel had asked. "What happens to them when you steal their medicine? What if they die? It's not my place to decide who lives and who dies, whose life has the greater value."

"But—those people are Barons. They're rich. They have everything they need!" the smuggler had argued.

"Maybe not," Samuel had said. "Not if they're unwilling to share with the poor. They need love, and they need compassion, and they need to know God. Stealing from them won't give them any of those things."

The smuggler had left shaking his head at Samuel's foolishness. Matthias thought maybe the smuggler had offered Samuel money too—money to feed himself and Percy and Alia. Matthias hadn't really understood. *If this safe contains medicine,* he told himself, still turning the lock, *I'm giving it to Percy and Alia. I don't care who else was supposed to have it.*

The lock clicked one final time, and Matthias jerked on the safe door. It actually opened an inch or so.

Medicine, medicine, medicine . . . , Matthias chanted to himself as he swung the safe door farther out.

Flat white plastic cards fell out on the ground.

Fake I.D.'s.

Matthias picked up one in disgust and threw it against the wall.

"I could make these myself, if I needed to," he muttered, and started to slam the door of the safe. Then he reconsidered. If someone found them hiding here in this secret room, they'd be in even bigger trouble if they didn't have identity cards. The identity cards could be "proof" that they weren't the three kids who had slipped away from the Population Police truck.

Matthias forced himself to slow down and search through the stack, until he found cards with pictures that bore some resemblance to himself and Percy and Alia. Most of the cards were for adults, so it took quite a while. By the time Matthias held three suitable I.D.'s in his hand, Percy was moaning.

"Over here, I think there's a cabin ahead. Oh no! Bullet! Shot! Climb hill! Hide!" he said, his voice crescendoing to a shriek. In his dreams, he seemed to be reliving the attack of the night before. He thrashed around on his bed so violently that Matthias feared he'd hurt himself even worse. Matthias put his hand on his friend's forehead, to calm him down and smooth the hair out of his face. But Percy's forehead was fiery hot; Matthias jerked his hand back as though Percy's skin could burn him.

"You've got a fever," Matthias said. "That's all. Just a little fever. I—" His voice shook. "I'm going upstairs to look for medicine there."

His legs trembled as he climbed the stairs and pushed up on the trapdoor. He was surprised by the bright sunlight that greeted him. It was still very early morning, but the woods outside the splintered door and broken windows seemed to sparkle. Percy's prediction had been right: It had snowed overnight.

Matthias refused to let himself be dazzled by the scene. He gingerly shut the trapdoor and focused his eyes on the ruined cabin.

It had probably not looked like much to begin with, but now it was a nightmarish place of overturned chairs and dark stains everywhere.

Bloodstains. Bloodstains from where seventeen rebels had fought and died.

Why didn't they just stay hidden in the secret underground room? Matthias wondered. But he thought he knew the answer. If they hadn't fought back, the Population Police would have come in and searched the place; they would have found the secret room anyway—and probably the safe with all the fake I.D.'s. The rebels had protected that room and that safe with their lives.

Was it worth it? Matthias wanted to know.

He went out and looked at the pile of bodies the

Population Police had made. With the dusting of snow on their clothes and faces, the bodies didn't look like real people anymore. They looked like statues or sculptures, somebody's twisted idea of art. The sign saying ENEMIES OF THE PEOPLE flapped in the breeze on a post beside the bodies.

Matthias had seen dead people before. He'd seen plenty of awful scenes when he'd lived in the city: children beaten by their parents, starving people screaming for food. But he'd had Samuel to protect him then—Samuel to protect him, and Percy and Alia to cuddle with at night. His life had been cozy in the midst of death and horror.

Now all that had been ripped away. The dead bodies seemed to stare at him, their tortured expressions seemed to whisper, *Percy will be joining us soon. Alia will be joining us soon. . . .*

"No!" Matthias screamed.

He whirled around and ran back into the cabin. He tore through it, ceiling to floor. He even searched between the cracks in the floor, in case some stray pills had fallen there. But the cabin contained no medicine. He had no way to help Percy and Alia. Not here.

"We'll leave, then," he muttered, lying on his stomach on the floor after searching the last crack. "We'll go somewhere else for help."

But he couldn't carry both of his friends at once. He'd barely managed to drag the two of them down the hill the night before.

He let his head fall, defeated, against the wood floor. His cheek rested against a bloodstain. Some people prayed this way, he remembered, their bodies absolutely flat on the ground. But Matthias wasn't praying. He was coming to terms with an awful truth.

I have to go away to get help for Percy and Alia, he thought. *I have to.*

But I have to leave them behind.

CHAPTER *TEN*

Matthias fed his friends before he left. He changed the makeshift bandages over their wounds—Percy's was soaked with blood, Alia's with yellowish pus. He tried to shake each of them awake, in turn, so he could explain what he was doing.

"It's too cold out there for the two of you," he choked out, trying to sound matter-of-fact. Trying to sound cheerful. "You get to stay in this nice, warm room and sleep all you want. Isn't that nice? I cut up some food and left it right here beside your beds. So you won't have to get up when you're hungry. And I'll leave the lantern burning. There's plenty of oil. Don't worry about anything—I'll be back soon. Very soon. With help."

Alia winced as if the sound of his voice pained her. Percy stared up glassy-eyed, then let his eyelids slip slowly down. Matthias couldn't be sure that either of them understood what he'd told them, but he didn't have time to wait around and try to explain some more. He didn't have the voice for it either. A huge lump seemed to have grown in his throat. He could barely breathe, let alone speak.

He ripped off a square section of a sheet, wrapped some of the remaining food in it, tied the corners together, and slung it over his shoulder. He climbed the ladder on unsteady legs. He carefully latched the trapdoor behind him, pausing only to admire the way the planks of the trapdoor fit perfectly into the rest of the floor. Invisibly.

Nobody could know the room is down there, he told himself. *It was just luck that I found it. Nobody will find Percy and Alia.*

He meant to run as soon as he got out of the door of the cabin, but he couldn't make himself hurry past the pile of dead bodies. The rattle of the ENEMIES OF THE PEOPLE sign against its post was too hypnotic and sad.

"You weren't enemies of the people, were you?" he whispered. The dead bodies stared back at him.

After a few seconds, Matthias jerked the sign down. He turned it over and went back into the cabin to get a pen. On the back of the sign, he wrote in big letters, THE POPU-LATION POLICE DID THIS.

He propped the sign up against the pile of dead bodies and slipped into the shadowy woods.

CHAPTER *ELEVEN*

Once, back at Niedler School, Matthias's history teacher had told a story about a soldier who ran twenty-five miles to tell his king about a victorious battle. The soldier covered all that distance at top speed, delivered his news, and immediately dropped over dead.

If this run is going to kill me, Matthias thought as he raced through the woods, *let me be like that soldier. Let me deliver my news first.*

Within a few minutes of leaving the cabin, Matthias got a stitch in his side. His feet got wet when he failed to see a stream until he was already in it. He could get his breath only in ragged gasps. But none of that worried him as much as the danger of being caught. He forced himself to slow down, look around, strive for silence.

Under different circumstances—if Percy and Alia were healthy and by his side, if he weren't worried about the Population Police chasing him—Matthias knew he could have appreciated his constantly changing view of the snowy woods. Samuel had taught the three kids to soak up beauty wherever they found it. But on this day, even the most beautiful trees were only obstacles and potential hiding places for enemies. The snow was only a threat: It melted into a wet, slippery mess as the day wore on, then turned to dangerous ice as evening approached. Matthias lost track of the number of times he slipped and fell. But he always forced himself back up onto his numb feet, forced himself to keep plodding onward.

By the time Matthias finally came in sight of Mr. Hendricks's cottage, it was night again and he was navigating by moonlight, straining his eyes just to see the road before him. Mr. Hendricks's windows let out a dim glow through drawn curtains, and Matthias stumbled toward that glow. He misjudged the size of the doorstep and careened directly into the side of the house.

"Who's there?" a voice called from inside, sharp and cautious. The glow in the windows immediately went dark. "Identify yourself."

"Ma—hias," Matthias mumbled. His tongue felt so swollen, he could barely say his own name. Odd—he couldn't remember stopping to take a drink of water even once the entire day. Maybe that was why he was having such trouble talking. Had he forgotten to eat, too? Maybe that was why he found himself sprawled on the ground, as if his spine and legs had given out at the same time.

A porch light clicked on.

"Matthias? Matthias, is that you?"

Someone opened the door and drew Matthias into the warmth. Someone shone a flashlight out into the darkness, searching.

"Matthias, what happened? Are you alone? Where are Percy and Alia?"

"Sick . . . hurt . . . go help them," Matthias managed to say. It was so tempting to give way to his exhaustion, even though he wasn't sure whether he'd fall asleep or die if he did. Maybe he would be like the marathon runner after all. But he hadn't delivered enough of his message yet. He hadn't told where Percy and Alia were.

"Cabin, big road," he mumbled.

"Matthias, for God's sake, just rest for a minute. You, John, go get him something to eat and drink—some broth, maybe?"

And probably Matthias did pass out then, because the next thing he knew he was lying in a huge bed. Mr. Hendricks was right beside his bed, spooning broth into his mouth. Mr. Hendricks's friend Mr. Talbot was there too, along with a red-haired woman and two young boys.

"He's not as bad as he looks. Most of the blood on his face and sweater isn't his. He's mostly just got scratches," the woman was saying. "Maybe a touch of frostbite on his feet too, but it's not bad."

"I'm fine. It's Percy and Alia—," Matthias struggled to say. The broth must have been helping because his tongue seemed to have returned to its usual size now. He found he could put words together in complete sentences again. "They're the ones to worry about."

"Hush," Mr. Hendricks said soothingly. "You don't have to tell us anything yet."

"Yes, I do!" Matthias sat up, even though Mr. Hendricks's hand was on his shoulder, trying to keep him still. Some of the broth spilled on the bed's comforter. "You've got to help Percy and Alia, not me!"

Matthias saw the grown-ups exchange troubled glances.

"Tell us, then," Mr. Hendricks said.

The whole story spilled out. At first the grown-ups interrupted with questions and comments. "The Population Police took away our students too, but they did that weeks ago," Mr. Hendricks said.

"Niedler is quite a bit farther out," Mr. Talbot said. "Do you suppose there are places they haven't reached yet?"

By the time Matthias began describing the massacre of the seventeen rebels, everyone was listening in silence.

"And after the Population Police left, I took Percy and Alia down into the cabin. There was a secret underground room, so I thought it was safe leaving them while I went for help. I didn't know what else to do. I couldn't carry them both. So, please, give me some medicine and tell me how to cure them and I'll go back right now and—"

"You're in no shape to go anywhere right now, young man," Mr. Hendricks said.

"But I've got to—"

"It doesn't have to be you who helps them," the red-haired woman said. She frowned. "I'll go."

"Theodora, no," Mr. Talbot said quickly. "You, alone, at night? That'd be like asking for—"

"I'm the only doctor here," the woman said sharply.

A doctor? Matthias felt better already.

"Let's discuss this elsewhere," Mr. Hendricks said, signaling with his eyes. "Let the boy rest while we figure out what to do. Joel, John, watch out for him. Keep feeding him."

Mr. Hendricks used a wheelchair, and there were times when that made him seem more powerful, more in control. This was one of those times. As Mr. Hendricks rolled out of the room on his bright silver wheels, it didn't seem like the grown-ups had any choice but to follow him; it didn't seem like the two boys half hiding at the foot of the bed had any choice but to shuffle up toward the head of the bed, to pick up the bowl and spoon Mr. Hendricks had left there.

But Matthias knew he had choices. As soon as the grown-ups shut the door behind them, he slipped out of bed, almost knocking over the other boys with their bowl of broth.

"What are you doing?" the one boy said. Matthias didn't know if it was Joel or John. He didn't care, either.

"Shh," he said.

He wobbled on his rubbery legs, but he made it to the door. He pressed his ear against the cool wood and listened for murmurings.

As he'd suspected, the grown-ups hadn't gone far for their discussion. They were right out in the hall.

"What are the chances that either of those children are still alive, even now?" Mr. Talbot was saying in a hushed voice.

"It sounds like the girl has a concussion and an infected wound," the woman's voice answered. "She should be okay, as long as the infection hasn't progressed too far. The boy—Percy?—I don't know. It depends on how the bullet went in, how much blood he's lost, how well Matthias managed to dress the wound. . . ."

"You think you have to go help them," Mr. Talbot said. It was a question without being a question.

"Well, of course, but—"

"You can't!" Mr. Talbot said. "The whole countryside's unstable, it'd be like walking through a minefield—I don't know how Matthias got here without being killed. If the mobs don't get you, the Population Police will."

"I'll drive," the woman said.

"Oh, that's a great idea. Why not just send out flares: 'I'm a Baron; I used to be richer than sin; I'm the very person you hate most!'"

"George, what if it were Jen, lying there in that cabin, on the verge of death? What if it were her and everyone refused to help?"

Mr. Talbot fell silent. Even Matthias knew who Jen was: She was Mr. Talbot's daughter, an illegal third child who'd been raised in luxury but who had died seeking her freedom.

She and Samuel had died together.

Through the door, Matthias heard Mr. Talbot take a ragged breath.

"Theodora, I just—I don't want to lose you, too."

"I know," the woman said softly. "But I have to go."

Matthias reached down and turned the doorknob. He jerked the door open.

"I'm going too," he said. "You're not leaving me behind."

The three grown-ups all startled at the sound of the door opening. Then Mr. Hendricks shook his head wryly.

"Theodora," he said, "I think you've got an assistant whether you like it or not."

CHAPTER *TWELVE*

To Matthias's way of thinking, the preparations for leaving took forever. Mrs. Talbot—for it turned out that's who Theodora was, Mr. Talbot's wife—had to pack bags of food and medicines and clothes. "In case we have to be there several days," she explained. "In case your friends can't be moved."

"Theodora doesn't travel light," Mr. Talbot said, attempting a chuckle that somehow turned into a stifled sob. He trailed his wife around the house as if he didn't want to let her out of his sight any sooner than he had to. "Maybe I should come too and—"

"George, you're a wanted man," Mrs. Talbot said sharply. "If they stop us and see you, that's it, we're all dead."

"Don't come," Matthias said.

He didn't understand how Mr. Talbot could be a wanted man, but it didn't matter. All Matthias cared about was getting back to his friends.

"And now we beat up the car," Mrs. Talbot said. "Want to help?"

"What?" Matthias asked, startled.

She led him to a shed behind Mr. Hendricks's house and flipped a switch. A long, elegant black car gleamed in the sudden light.

"If the mobs stop us, we want them to think we stole this car," Mrs. Talbot said. "If the Population Police detain us, we want it to look like we've fallen on hard times. Either way, this car is too . . . perfect."

She grabbed a sledgehammer that was leaning against the wall and aimed it at the center of the hood.

"I can't watch," Mr. Talbot said.

Matthias decided he couldn't either. But ten minutes later, when Mrs. Talbot backed the car out of the shed, it looked more like a crumbled heap of scrap metal than a drivable vehicle.

"Don't worry, dear," Mrs. Talbot told her husband, leaning out the window. "It's only cosmetic damage. If I make it back here, you can spend the whole winter fixing it up."

"Don't say that," Mr. Talbot said. "Don't you know how hard this is for me already?"

"Now you know how I felt all those years, watching you head off into danger," Mrs. Talbot said.

Matthias climbed into the passenger side of the car. Mr. and Mrs. Talbot were kissing each other good-bye now, and he had no desire to watch that.

Mr. Hendricks rolled out toward them, and Joel and John walked behind him.

"Be careful," Mr. Hendricks said.

"Of course," Mrs. Talbot said. She rolled up her window and put her foot on the accelerator, and they zipped past the others. "I hate good-byes," she said.

Mrs. Talbot barely slowed down as they approached the end of the driveway.

"Which way?" she asked impatiently.

"Turn right," Matthias said. "And then left at the next intersection. The cabin's on the main road into those woods, about halfway in, I think, right after the stream."

He wished they could get there as quickly as he could give directions. Mrs. Talbot seemed to feel the same way. She sped around the corner, then pressed the accelerator to the floor. They went faster and faster; everything outside the window blurred before Matthias's eyes.

"We need to get our stories straight, in case anyone stops us," Mrs. Talbot said grimly, keeping her gaze straight ahead. She clutched the steering wheel with both hands. "I'm your mother, and I'm taking you to Population Police headquarters so you can join up."

"Join the Population Police? Why would I do that?" Matthias asked, recoiling from her words.

Mrs. Talbot sighed and glanced his way quickly before staring back at the road before them.

"I guess you didn't hear all the news lately, out at Niedler," she said. "The Population Police issued an edict that nobody but them is allowed to sell food. And nobody can buy food unless at least one member of the family is part of the Population Police."

"Oh," Matthias said. All of that seemed horribly remote to him. The car was warm—even his seat seemed to be breathing heat around him. It made him sleepy. He forced himself to stay alert. He remembered something. "When the Population Police came to Niedler, they said that the Government had a new leader and that was why we had to go to the work camp."

Mrs. Talbot sighed again, even more heavily this time.

"Yes," she said. "The leader of the Population Police took over the whole country. Aldous Krakenaur. The Population Police are in control of everything now."

"That doesn't matter," Matthias said.

"What?" Mrs. Talbot asked. She seemed so stunned that she almost drove off the road. She had to jerk violently on the steering wheel to get the car back on course.

Matthias shrugged.

"What's the difference?" he asked. "Samuel—the man who raised us—he said that governments will rise and governments will fall, and man will do evil to man, and all we can do is turn our hearts to good."

"Well, that's certainly a broad view of things," Mrs. Talbot muttered.

"Samuel didn't believe in getting involved in politics," Matthias said. He frowned in the darkness, remembering the one time Samuel had seemed to go against his own principles. "But when there was that rally for the rights of third children back in April . . . Samuel went to that. I've never understood why. That's where he died."

Mrs. Talbot was silent for a moment, and Matthias was afraid he'd upset her by talking about the rally where her own daughter had died. Trees flashed by in the darkness.

"I know who your Samuel was, then," Mrs. Talbot finally said. "George got . . . tapes of the rally. Because of Jen. Samuel was the old man with the long beard who went right up to the Population Police while they were shooting and told them, 'These are innocent children. What you're doing is a sin and an abomination.'"

Matthias hadn't known that. He hadn't really known how Samuel had died.

"But did it do any good?" Matthias asked. "They still killed all the children. And Samuel." Matthias barely knew Mrs. Talbot. But somehow, in the dark, it seemed safe to confide in her. "Samuel always said everything happens for a reason. But what could have been the reason for him to die?"

"I don't know," Mrs. Talbot said. "But you shouldn't think that he died in vain. After he was shot, some of the Population Police turned their guns on one another. There was . . . almost a mutiny in the ranks. I didn't know about it for weeks afterward. But for a long time, that was the only thing that gave me enough hope to go on living."

Matthias closed his eyes. This was too much to absorb, too much to think about when he was so tired and so worried about Percy and Alia.

"I know what it's like to live without hope," Mrs. Talbot said. "When we lost Jen . . . When I thought George was doomed as well . . . These are uncertain times we live in. But your Samuel was wrong if he thought it doesn't matter who's in charge of the Government. There is reason to hope for an end to all this evil. I believe it's your generation that will win the cause. . . ."

She started telling him a long story about how a group of other kids had joined the Population Police just to sabotage it, to fight the organization's evil from inside. Her story was interesting, but her voice was so lulling and the car was so warm and the sound of the wheels on the road so soothing that Matthias slipped straight into sleep.

When he woke up, the car was stopped.

"You have impeccable timing," Mrs. Talbot told him. "Incredibly enough, we made it here safely."

The headlights of the car shone on the side of the cabin.

"How'd you know this was the right place?" Matthias asked.

"That," Mrs. Talbot said grimly, pointing at the pile of dead bodies off to the right. She shut off the headlights, turned off the car, and picked up her bag of medicines. "Maybe I should go in first, just to see."

Matthias suspected she was trying to protect him, in case Percy and Alia hadn't survived the hours he'd been away.

"No," he said quickly, picking up a flashlight. "You'll need me to show you how to open the trapdoor."

Mrs. Talbot didn't object. They both got out of the car, and the chilly night air was all Matthias needed to come fully awake.

"Don't look at the bloodstains," he told Mrs. Talbot as they stepped through the shattered doorway into the cabin.

"I've seen blood before," Mrs. Talbot said.

The circle of the flashlight's glow was eerie against the plank floor because of the blood and the shadows of all the cracks. Matthias was eager to get down to the secret room and the lantern's cozy light. He found the latch quickly and lifted the trapdoor.

"Percy? Alia?" he called softly. "I got help, just like I promised."

The lantern had gone out, but that didn't faze him. He climbed down the ladder and pointed his flashlight upward so Mrs. Talbot could see to climb down as well. Then he turned the light toward the cots. The glow was so feeble that it didn't penetrate very far into the darkness. He couldn't see. . . . He stepped closer. He could make out the frames of the cots, the blankets piled on top of them— the empty cots, the folded blankets.

Percy and Alia were gone.

CHAPTER THIRTEEN

Where are they?" Mrs. Talbot asked, looking around.

She didn't understand that they were missing. Matthias couldn't understand either. He whipped the flashlight all around, and its glow shot crazily from one side of the room to the other. Maybe Percy and Alia had crawled off their cots to go to the bathroom and then fainted before they could get back. . . . Maybe that might have happened to one of them, but both?

Neither of them was huddled anywhere on the secret room's dirt floor. They'd vanished completely.

Matthias raced back up the ladder. Maybe they were in the cabin itself. . . .

He repeated his routine of flashing the light all around the room. The upturned chairs made shadows big enough to hide behind, so he kept getting glimmers of hope— hope that died instantly when he moved the chairs aside and saw nothing there. He scrambled to the door of the cabin.

"Percy? Alia?" he shouted hoarsely into the dark night. "Where are you?"

Mrs. Talbot grabbed his arm just as he started to step outside to search for them.

"Are you out of your mind?" she asked, her eyes blazing. "Are you trying to find them or get us killed?"

If he couldn't find Percy and Alia, it would be like dying.

"They were here," he said furiously. "What could have happened to them? I never should have left them. This is all my fault. It's my fault Percy got shot—the Population Police must have heard him answering me. It's my fault Alia got hurt—oh, why didn't I think before I tried to stop that truck? Why didn't I—?"

"Stop it," Mrs. Talbot said, taking him by the shoulders and shaking him. "Hysteria never helped anyone. We can look for them, we can find them if you'll just calm down."

"Somebody took them away," Matthias moaned.

"Yes, probably," Mrs. Talbot agreed. "From your description of their injuries, I don't think they could have walked out of here on their own. We just need to figure out who took them and why. . . . I know. You go back down into the basement and see if there are any secret routes out that you missed before. I'll go outside and look for footprints."

Matthias had searched the underground room as thoroughly as possible the night before, so he didn't think much of Mrs. Talbot's suggestion. But he didn't say so. He sat numbly until she was out the door. Then he sneaked over and watched her.

She kept her flashlight trained on the ground for only a few moments. Then, when she reached the pile of dead bodies, she pointed the light straight at it.

She believes Percy and Alia might be dead, Matthias thought, so jarred by the thought that he staggered backward. *She thinks someone just threw their bodies on the pile with the others.*

He heard Mrs. Talbot gasp, and he ran outside to join her.

"Is it Percy? Alia?" he asked.

Mrs. Talbot glanced over at him like she'd forgotten who he was.

"No . . . no," she murmured. "There aren't any children here. But it's . . . someone I used to know. The man who sold us our daughter's fake identity card." She took Matthias's flashlight from him and switched it off. "This is too strange. Nothing makes sense. Let's go search the underground room together and wait until daylight before we look for footprints. These flashlights are too much like beacons in the dark."

"But—," Matthias started to object. He thought they'd find his friends fastest by following footprints.

"I insist," Mrs. Talbot said. "It's only about twenty minutes or so until sunrise."

Troubled, Matthias followed Mrs. Talbot back into the cabin and down the stairs. The two of them tapped on the walls and floors for what felt like hours, but no secret tunnels or hideaways appeared. Matthias showed her the safe that had contained all the false identity cards.

"Do you remember the combination?" Mrs. Talbot asked.

"Um, I think so," Matthias said. It took him a few tries, but he finally got the safe open.

It was empty too.

"So they took two injured children and dozens of fake I.D.'s," Mrs. Talbot said. "Hmm."

"What?" Matthias asked. "What do you think happened?"

"I don't know," Mrs. Talbot said. She gave him a shaky smile. "Got any guesses?"

Matthias wished he were as smart as Percy. Percy would have been able to look at the clues they had and come up with a solid answer: *Oh, yes, they left with a man in a gray hat, and the serial number on his I.D. card ends in two-three, and we'll find them if we travel north by northeast for forty-five minutes.*

Okay, maybe Percy wouldn't be able to figure out that much detail. *But if it were Percy looking for Alia and me, not the other way around,* Matthias thought, *he'd know enough to tell for sure if the Population Police had come back and discovered the secret room and the fake I.D.'s and his friends. . . . Oh, please, God, don't let it be the Population Police who found them.*

Matthias gulped. "Let's go see if we can find any footprints," he told Mrs. Talbot.

She shrugged and followed him back up the ladder yet again. They closed the trapdoor behind them.

Dim light was filtering into the cabin from outdoors now. It only served to highlight the disarray. Mrs. Talbot stood at the splintered door and peeked outside.

"When it's dark out," she murmured, "I'm always terrified of what might be hiding in the shadows. But when the sun comes up, I wish for the darkness again to hide me."

Matthias brushed past her. It didn't do any good to speak of fear.

He took a few steps toward the road and then looked back. He'd left no footprints in the leaf-strewn, packed dirt. He shivered, but his chill had nothing to do with the brisk morning air.

Maybe whoever took Percy and Alia away was here yesterday when the ground thawed and then refroze, he told himself. *So their footprints might still be there, encrusted in the ground, even though I can't see my own.*

He peered around, his gaze taking in the sky and the woods as well as the ground.

And that was when he saw the man in the tree.

CHAPTER *FOURTEEN*

Really, Matthias could see only eyes and maybe a dark boot in the shadows of one of the trees across the road. But the eyes were focused precisely.

Watching Matthias.

Alia would have seen him before I did, before he saw her, Matthias thought shakily. *She would have known not to step out of the cabin.*

But Matthias didn't have Alia with him, and he barely knew what to do without her and Percy making decisions with him. At least the man wasn't doing anything but watching. He didn't swing down from the tree, didn't dash across the road to attack. Matthias dropped to the ground and pretended that he had to tie his shoe.

"Mrs. Talbot!" he hissed urgently, his head bent down so the man wouldn't be able to see his lips moving. "Stay in the cabin. Someone's watching."

She didn't answer, but she didn't step out of the cabin either.

Matthias took his time fiddling with his shoelaces. Surely the man knew that Matthias had seen him. Surely if the man was going to harm Matthias, he would have already done it.

Could he be . . . a helper? Matthias wondered. *On our side?*

He stood up, his heart thumping hard, a risky plan forming in his mind.

"Percy? Alia?" he called. "Are you close by?"

He fixed his gaze on the eyes in the tree across the road. They bobbed up and down, once. Was that a nod? Did the man know what had happened to Matthias's friends? Had the man himself taken them?

"Are they safe?" Matthias called again, his voice hoarse.

Again, the eyes moved, in concert. Down, up, down, up. Dead brown leaves rustled around the eyes; Matthias saw a hand reach out and pull back. The man was holding up one finger. He put the finger against lips and a beard that appeared briefly in a gap in the leaves.

"You want me to be quiet?" Matthias asked.

Another nod.

The arm emerged from the branches once more. The man seemed to be waving at Matthias now—waving or trying to shove leaves out of his way.

Matthias didn't understand.

"What?" he half whispered. "Can't you just come down and tell me what—"

The finger went back to the lips, and Matthias broke off. The arm waved again and pointed off to the east.

Matthias went and stood in the middle of the road. He squinted straight down the road toward the rising sun but could see nothing unusual. He turned and walked toward the man's tree.

The man's waves became frantic now, and Matthias could understand this gesture. It meant: *Go back! Get away from here!*

"Well, all right, if that's how you want it," Matthias muttered. None of this made sense to him, but he obediently backed away from the man's tree. He considered going back into the cabin to confer with Mrs. Talbot, but he didn't want to let the man out of his sight. And he couldn't be sure the man was an ally; he didn't want to expose Mrs. Talbot to any danger. If he'd had Percy and Alia with him, the three of them could have made a split-second decision. Alone, Matthias could only stand in the middle of the road, his face scrunched up in bafflement, his feet turned halfway between coming and going.

So that's where Matthias was when the four Population Police officers burst out of the woods to the east.

CHAPTER *FIFTEEN*

Halt!" the lead officer yelled, even though Matthias clearly wasn't moving. "Who are you? What are you doing here?"

Matthias gaped at them. *Look surprised but innocent,* he told himself. He made himself blink once or twice, slowly. He let them march right up to him.

"I—," he started. "I was just—"

He had to work so hard to keep from glancing over at the man in the tree. He didn't want to give the man away.

"Just what?" the officer demanded. He stepped closer to Matthias and glared down his nose.

Then, before Matthias had a chance to answer, a flurry of gunshots rained down on the four Population Police officers. Three of them fell instantly, but the fourth, the one closest to Matthias, had time to pull a gun out of his shirt. He dived behind Mrs. Talbot's car and began returning fire.

And Matthias, standing by himself out in the open in

the middle of the gun battle, suddenly understood. The man in the tree had been waiting to ambush the Population Police. He'd been trying to get Matthias out of the way so Matthias wouldn't get hurt too.

Matthias turned, ready to run back for the safety of the cabin. Then he froze. Mrs. Talbot was in the cabin. What if he led the Population Police right to her? What if the Population Police officer killed the man in the tree? What would happen to Percy and Alia then?

Matthias veered away from the cabin and slid down behind the front bumper of Mrs. Talbot's car. He slithered over to the Population Police officer.

"There are dozens of them!" he whispered in the officer's ear. "They're circling around behind us. Get in the car!"

The officer gave him a startled look, but when Matthias opened the car door, the officer slipped through it. Matthias shoved him on over to the passenger side and slid into the driver's seat.

The Population Police officer and the man in the tree were still shooting at each other. Matthias ducked down low, twisting wires together and praying. He'd seen other boys on the street hot-wire cars. He'd never actually done it himself before, but maybe, maybe . . .

The engine roared to life, and Matthias stomped on the accelerator. He had to stretch his leg out as far as he could, and still his toes barely touched the pedal. But the car lurched forward. At the last minute, Matthias managed to swerve to miss the side of the cabin, and a few final bullets pinged off the back of the car.

And then they were out of range of the man in the tree.

The Population Police officer still kept his gun trained toward the woods. He fired over Matthias's head, shattering the window. Shards of glass rained down on Matthias, but he only ducked down lower and pressed the accelerator harder. He heard an angry squawk off to the side, behind them.

"Oh," the officer muttered. "That one was just a bird."

The officer let his body sag back against the leather seat. Matthias could see the beads of sweat along his hairline.

"You . . . saved . . . my life," the officer whispered.

Matthias hadn't thought of it that way. He felt more like he'd been involved in a kidnapping. He kept his foot on the accelerator, putting even more distance between them and the cabin.

"That's . . . not how it usually works," the officer said. He sounded dazed. "Population Police officers are supposed to fight to the death. Never give up."

"I don't see how it would have hurt the, uh, bad guys if you died," Matthias said, because he had to say something. It was strange talking to someone he might have wished dead a few minutes earlier.

The officer wiped the sweat off his face with the back of his hand.

"I could say I made an executive decision to go back for reinforcements," he mused. "Since there were so many rebels." For a minute, Matthias feared that the officer was making fun of Matthias's lie: *There are dozens of them. . . .* But the officer's expression was serious. Matthias remembered how the bullets had seemed to come all at once. *Maybe there really were other men in other trees,* he thought.

"Let me drive now," the officer ordered.

Matthias took his foot off the accelerator. He had to slide practically his whole body down under the steering wheel to reach the brake. It was a good thing he hadn't needed to stop quickly.

The officer slid over into the driver's seat, and Matthias opened the door and circled around behind the battered car.

I could take off running into the woods now, Matthias thought. *But would the officer chase me? Would I put Percy and Alia and Mrs. Talbot and the man in the tree in even more danger?*

The officer still had his gun; he was watching Matthias in the rearview mirror. Matthias got back into the car on the passenger's side.

What will Mrs. Talbot do without her car? he wondered. *Will she and the man in the tree find each other now that the Population Police are out of the way? What if the man in the tree was lying about Percy and Alia being safe?*

Not knowing made Matthias ache all over. *Oh, God, protect Alia, oh, God, protect Percy* kept running through his mind, to the same rhythm as the wheels.

The Population Police officer was still watching Matthias, glancing back and forth between Matthias and the road ahead.

"You know, you never did answer my questions," the officer said. He was going very fast now, much faster than Matthias would have dared to drive. He kept one hand on the steering wheel and one hand on his gun.

"Questions?" Matthias repeated.

"Why were you standing there in the middle of the road?"

"Oh, I was just passing by," Matthias said vaguely.

"Passing by? Out here in the middle of nowhere?"

Matthias heard the suspicion in the officer's voice; he saw the officer's blue eyes narrow and his mouth harden into a distrustful line. And Matthias couldn't help watching the gun. The officer wasn't pointing it toward the woods anymore. He had the barrel turned almost casually toward Matthias.

The only thing Matthias could think of was the story Mrs. Talbot had concocted.

"I was on my way to join the Population Police," Matthias squeaked.

The officer laughed, giving off a great guffaw that seemed to roar through the entire car.

"You? What are you—six? Seven? Eight? Granted, I've been away from headquarters for a while, but last time I checked, we weren't signing up kindergartners."

Matthias drew himself up to his full height, which admittedly wasn't much.

"I'm thirteen," he said in what he hoped was a dignified voice. He didn't know why he picked that age—he didn't know if the Population Police were any more likely to accept thirteen-year-olds than eleven-year-olds, the age he'd given the last time anyone had asked, back at Niedler School. But he felt like he'd aged a lot in the last few days. He felt thirteen.

It was an unlucky number, after all.

The Population Police officer was studying Matthias's face.

"My apologies, then," he muttered. He stopped the car and turned to face Matthias directly. The gun went back down to his side. "Who am I to question the young man who saved my life? I can't imagine any better start to a Population Police career than the one you just had. In fact, I'll induct you right now. What's your name?"

Matthias had to struggle to remember the name on the fake I.D. he'd taken from the safe in the cabin.

"Uh, Roger Symmes," he said.

"Well, then, Roger Symmes, I hereby inaugurate you into the grand tradition of the Population Police. I believe you're already in line for a medal for meritorious service. Congratulations." He reached over and shook Matthias's hand. And, for a final touch, he took off his own official Population Police cap and settled it on Matthias's head. It was much too large and slipped down, almost entirely covering his eyes.

And Matthias, in the midst of still praying, *Oh, God, protect Alia, oh, God, protect Percy,* had to force himself not to flinch at the touch of the Population Police officer, of the Population Police cap.

Oh, God, can you protect me, too? he wondered.

CHAPTER SIXTEEN

The Population Police officer seemed to have satisfied all his doubts about Matthias now. He tucked his gun away out of sight before pressing his foot down on the accelerator again.

"My name's Tidwell, by the way," the officer said. "Friends call me 'Tiddy.'"

"Tiddy"? Matthias thought. *The big, fierce Population Police officer goes by "Tiddy"?*

Without his official cap, Tiddy looked younger, almost boyish himself. His blond hair was cut very short, with razor-sharp precision, and his uniform was still crisply pressed, even after the march through the woods and the surprise attack. But he didn't have the cold, steely-eyed look of all the other Population Police Matthias had ever seen.

"Um, Tiddy?" Matthias asked. "Where are we going?"

"Back to HQ," Tiddy said. "Headquarters. You'll get your assignment—further assignment, I should say—and I'll put in orders for those reinforcements." He was silent for a minute, then added, "Wish you'd been able to save Hathaway, Grimes, and Sully, too."

Matthias guessed he meant the other three Population Police, the men who had died in the first hail of gunfire.

"Were they your friends?" Matthias asked.

"Yes," Tiddy said softly, his eyes carefully trained on the road ahead. "They were."

It was strange for Matthias to think of Tiddy, a Population Police officer, missing his friends just as Matthias was worrying about Percy and Alia.

"You should know," Tiddy went on, so quietly that he almost seemed to be talking to himself, "being in the Population Police is a dangerous business. It's not just about privileges and promotions. We're serving the cause and . . . not everybody understands."

"The cause?" Matthias asked.

Tiddy glanced over at him.

"You're thirteen, huh?" Tiddy said. "That's too young to remember the famines. I was just a boy myself then, not much older than you. We'd always had food. Back then, you could go into a grocery store and there'd be aisles and aisles of every food you could imagine. Even meat—I bet you've never tasted meat in your entire life, have you?"

Matthias shook his head. No. Of course he'd never tasted meat.

"They had these things called cheeseburgers. . . . Well, never mind. The point is, everyone had plenty of food. You didn't really think about it. You just ate. And then it stopped raining. It didn't rain *ever*. I wasn't really paying attention, I was just a kid, but the newspeople were always on TV blathering on about 'The droughts! The droughts! What if the rains never come back?' This is awful, but me and my friends, we used to laugh about it. It was like the grown-ups telling themselves horror stories, trying to scare themselves. Nobody was *really* worried. But then those grocery store shelves started emptying out, and people started fighting over what food there was. . . . Everybody would have starved if it hadn't been for the Population Police."

Matthias had heard a story sort of like this from Samuel. But in Samuel's version, told beside a small fire in the dark tunnel, he always ended by musing, "Was this a judgment on our wickedness, O Lord?"

And in Samuel's tale, the Population Police were part of the evil visited on the land, not the people's salvation.

"How did the Population Police keep people from starving?" Matthias asked.

"You don't know?" Tiddy asked. He shook his head in disbelief. "Look at it this way. If you've got one box of rice and ten thousand people, nobody's going to survive. But if you've got only ten people, everyone gets a bellyful. The Population Police just make sure there aren't too many people. It's, like, simple math."

Not so simple if you're one of the people who are "too many," Matthias thought.

"What's amazing," Tiddy continued, "is how people try to get around the rules. Rules that are there for their own good! You know what was happening back at that cabin? People were making fake I.D.'s so they could get extra food. And then they were so greedy that they fought about it and started shooting one another—that's why there were all those bodies by the side of the road. The Population Police, we were just going in to clean up the mess. But not only did the rebels start shooting at us, did you see that sign? By the bodies? Somebody wrote, 'The Population Police did this'—like they were trying to blame everything on us. Lies, lies, lies. It's just so wrong!"

Matthias froze. Did Tiddy have any idea who had written that sign? No—Tiddy was banging his hand on the steering wheel and his voice cracked with indignation, but he was also nodding his head toward Matthias, like he thought Matthias was completely on his side. An ally. (Well, hadn't Matthias acted like he was—saving Tiddy's life, shaking hands over the notion of joining the Population Police? Why would Tiddy suspect Matthias of anything?)

Something else struck Matthias: Tiddy seemed to truly believe that the rebels, not the Population Police, had killed those seventeen people.

Matthias opened his mouth. Then closed it. He couldn't very well tell Tiddy, *But you're the one who's wrong! I was there the night before last! I saw the Population Police kill the rebels!* He

MARGARET PETERSON HADDIX

closed his eyes and leaned his head back against the seat.

"I know," Tiddy said sympathetically. "It's almost too much to bear, isn't it?"

They drove the rest of the way without much conversation. Matthias was worrying about Percy and Alia, and he suspected that Tiddy was grieving for his friends. Matthias watched the scenery flash by—first the country-side, with scant villages, then the streets of a large city Matthias didn't recognize. He paid close attention. He wanted to memorize the route so he could slip away and hike back to the cabin as soon as possible.

But when they got to Population Police headquarters— a monstrous building surrounded by a towering stone fence—he was chilled by the sight of guards everywhere. Hordes of them stood by the fence, by the gate, by every door and window. After Tiddy drove in past a guardhouse, a line of guards closed in across the road as quickly as a prison door slamming shut.

Oh, Percy, Matthias thought, as if his friend could really hear him, all those miles away, *even you couldn't escape from this place.*

CHAPTER SEVENTEEN

Tiddy parked the car at a reckless angle and hollered over to one of the guards by the front door, "Hey, fill out the paperwork on this car for me, will you? We requisitioned it from the enemy. It didn't come with a key."

Some of the guards chuckled, and Matthias heard one of them snort, "That's Tiddy for you."

"Come on, kid. You stick with me," Tiddy said to Matthias as they got out of the car.

"You requisition the kid, too?" one of the guards teased.

"Nope. He saved my life," Tiddy said, bounding up to the door.

"Yeah, sure," the guards muttered. "Can't wait to hear that story."

Matthias followed Tiddy into the imposing headquarters building and through a maze of halls and stairs the way he had once followed Samuel through the reeking, trash-strewn streets of his city. He didn't feel like he had much choice. It seemed like he'd cast his fate with Tiddy's when he'd shoved the officer into Mrs. Talbot's car. And, strangely, staying close to Tiddy helped staunch the fear pounding in his head: *This is Population Police headquarters! Everyone here is evil!*

Then a guard standing before an interior door in a grand hallway planted himself firmly in front of Matthias, blocking his way.

"Officer Tidwell!" the guard chided, cutting his eyes disdainfully toward Matthias. "Surely you understand that it wouldn't be proper—"

"Proper?" Tiddy looked from the guard to Matthias. "Oh, relax. This is our newest Population Police member. He's been too busy perpetrating acts of heroism to get his uniform yet."

"Still, to go in there—," the guard persisted.

"Oh, very well," Tiddy said. "Send for a uniform. Size extra small."

Tiddy waited with Matthias until someone came with a uniform. It was gray, not black like Tiddy's. And it was at least three sizes too big.

"That's the best they can do down in the uniform room?" Tiddy asked, glancing at the sizing tag. "Oh, well. Just put it on over your clothes. You could use the extra bulk."

Matthias pulled the pants over his pajama bottoms. He had to make an extra hole in the belt to get them to stay up. He stuck his arm into the first sleeve. His sweater bunched up and rubbed uncomfortably.

Oh no, he thought. *I was planning to give Alia my sweater, way back before Percy was shot. . . .* In his rush to find shelter, tend his friends' wounds, and go for help, he'd totally forgotten. *What if the man in the tree didn't take Alia someplace warm? What if she freezes to death because of me?*

Matthias's knees threatened to give out at this horrible thought. He sagged back against the doorway.

Tiddy gently pulled the uniform shirt the rest of way around Matthias's body. He pushed Matthias's other arm through the other sleeve.

"You don't have to button it," Tiddy said. "Come on, it's time to see the commander."

Numbly, Matthias followed Tiddy past the guard and through a doorway that seemed, just by itself, to be taller and wider than most normal houses. The room beyond was so vast and awe-inspiring that Matthias came to a dead halt. A row of ornate chairs led up to a wooden desk that seemed as big as a car. The windows—all ten of them—stretched from the floor to the ceiling and were studded with colored glass.

And between the windows were black banners, just as tall and even wider—banners showing children dying, Population Police officers cheering.

It's like a cathedral, Matthias thought dizzily. *A cathedral where people worship evil.*

"Sir!" Tiddy was saying, snapping his arm into a salute.

Belatedly, Matthias thought he ought to salute too. He lifted his arm, and the excess material of his uniform sleeve swung against his cap, knocking it off. Tiddy noticed and swung his hand down, smoothly catching the cap before it hit the floor. And, in spite of the fact that Tiddy was a Population Police officer and therefore Matthias's worst enemy, Matthias felt a surge of gratitude.

"At ease. Approach," a creaky old voice said from the far end of the room.

Tiddy and Matthias walked past all the empty chairs, toward the massive desk. The oldest man Matthias had ever seen in his entire life was sitting behind it.

"I am saddened to report the loss of my men, Commander," Tiddy said.

The old man looked down at a paper on his desk.

"That would be Sullivan, Grimes, and Hathaway?"

"Yes, sir."

The old man—the commander—bent over and slowly made three notations on his paper.

"Explain," he said.

"We were patrolling in the endangered territories," Tiddy said. "We had just come across this boy"—he pointed toward Matthias—"who was journeying to enlist in the Population Police. And then suddenly we were set upon by the enemy. There must have been thirty or forty of them, at least. All armed."

Thirty or forty? Matthias thought. *How could that be?* He knew for sure of only one man in one tree.

"Sullivan, Grimes, and Hathaway were murdered in the first strike," Tiddy continued.

"Indeed," the commander said. "And how is it that you escaped?"

Matthias wondered if Tiddy would lie about that as well. But Tiddy turned and pointed to Matthias again.

"This boy—this, this *hero*—he contrived a plan to steal us away to safety in a requisitioned car. We've come for reinforcements."

"Ah," the commander said. He leaned back in his vast leather chair and focused his attention on Matthias.

"How many of the enemy did you see, young man?" he asked.

Matthias forced himself to stare straight back at the commander. But what was he supposed to say? He didn't want to lie or even to back up Tiddy's lies indirectly. But he felt a strange sort of loyalty to Tiddy.

"I don't know, sir," Matthias finally said. "They were hiding. There were a lot of bullets, though."

"Cowards," the commander said, biting off the word as if it left a horrible taste in his mouth.

"You see the blood on his sweater, sir," Tiddy said. "It was mayhem."

And then Matthias had to choke back his anger. The blood on his sweater was from carrying an injured Alia, from tending Percy's gunshot wounds. As far as Matthias was concerned, those bloodstains were practically sacred.

But the commander didn't even look. He was sliding papers around on his desk.

"You'll get your troops," he told Tiddy. "Dismissed."

"Thank you, sir," Tiddy said

He turned and strode away from the commander, down the aisle with all the empty chairs. Matthias had to rush to keep up with him. Out in the hall, Tiddy winked at Matthias.

"That went well, don't you think?" he said.

Matthias waited until they were several paces past the snooty guard. He glanced around to make sure there was no one else within earshot. Then he said quietly, "There weren't forty people shooting at us."

Tiddy shrugged and kept walking. "Sometimes you have to exaggerate a little to get the commander's attention. Besides, how are you so sure there weren't forty? Or fifty? I don't know about you, but I didn't have time to stop and count. Twenty, forty, fifty, a hundred—who cares? This way, I know the commander will give me enough men to take care of the problem in that sector."

Problem? Matthias thought. He was pretty sure Percy and Alia were hiding out with the "problem." What would happen to them? How could Matthias possibly help them when he was stuck at Population Police headquarters and they were so far away?

And then Matthias knew.

"Are you going back right now?" Matthias asked. "I want to come too!"

Tiddy laughed.

"You're an eager one, aren't you?" he asked. "Much as I'd

appreciate having you around to watch my back—or steal cars for me—I don't think there's any way I could get approval to take a new recruit with me into *that* sector."

"But I was just there!" Matthias argued desperately. "What's the difference?"

"Procedure," Tiddy said with a shrug. "Got to follow the rules, you know?"

They were descending a set of stairs, then stringing their way through an array of twisty hallways. Finally they came out in front of another huge door in the middle of a bustling lobby.

"Give yourself six months, maybe a year," Tiddy said. "I'll make sure you're signed up for all the necessary training. If you do well, and if we still have enemies left to fight then, I promise, I'll take you with me every battle I can."

"But—," Matthias protested. Where would Percy and Alia be in six months or a year?

"No 'but's' about it," Tiddy said. "Now, I have to go back to the field, and you get to have a delicious meal courtesy of the Population Police. Honestly, I think you're getting the better end of the deal."

He led Matthias through the doorway, which opened into a huge eating area. Dozens of uniformed men, women, and teenagers were sitting at long tables, hunched over trays. And there were all sorts of heady aromas in the air: freshly baked breads, simmering stews, baked potatoes. . . . In spite of his worries, Matthias couldn't help closing his eyes and inhaling deeply.

"I knew you'd like this part," Tiddy said, chuckling.

He said something to a woman sitting at the end of a serving line at the side of the room, and the woman handed Matthias a tray.

"Fill up your stomach, and I'll check up on you when I get back," Tiddy said. *"Ciao!"*

Matthias stood there numbly, watching Tiddy walk away.

What do I do now? he wondered. He wanted to chase after Tiddy, but that wouldn't do any good if Tiddy wouldn't take him back to the cabin.

If only Percy and Alia were here to help me think . . . Matthias remembered a story Samuel had told him about a strong man who lost all his strength when his hair was cut off. That man had been captured by his enemies too. Matthias felt just as weak and stupid and useless without his friends. How was he ever going to escape from Population Police headquarters and get back to Percy and Alia?

"Bean soup, sir?" someone asked.

Matthias swayed a little. He was hungry. Starving, actually. He hadn't eaten since—when? The broth back at Mr. Hendricks's house? That seemed like several lifetimes ago. Would it be so awful to eat something now, so he'd have energy to think of a plan?

"Okay," Matthias said.

A woman placed a steaming bowl of soup on his tray. Another woman put a plateful of rolls beside the soup, and a girl added a cup of mixed fruit.

Matthias hadn't seen fruit like that in ages, and he loved it.

"Thank you," he said, looking straight at the girl. And then he looked again. The girl had a white papery hat covering her hair and a sanitary mask covering her nose and mouth, but there was something oddly familiar about her brown eyes. She looked like . . . No, she was—

"Nina?" Matthias whispered.

CHAPTER *EIGHTEEN*

The serving girl scowled at Matthias and shook her head—just once, forbiddingly.

"Keep it moving," she said in a harsh tone that didn't disguise the familiar voice.

Matthias wanted to scream out, *Nina! What are you doing here?* and *Please, can you help me get back to Percy and Alia?* But he said nothing, only picked up his tray and walked away. He aimed for a table on the far side of the room, where he could sit alone with his back toward the wall.

Where he could watch Nina.

Nina had escaped from Population Police prison with him and Percy and Alia months ago. She'd started at Niedler School when they did but had been called away in early October. Mr. Hendricks needed her help, she'd told them, sounding a little self-important. What was she doing working for the Population Police now? Had Matthias and his friends come to the wrong conclusion about her loyalties— had she been on the Population Police's side all along?

Matthias remembered he was wearing a Population Police uniform himself. What if she'd met a fate similar to his, where she'd had to pretend to be on the Population Police's side to protect somebody else?

Then Matthias remembered something Mrs. Talbot had said in the car, in the dark on the way to the cabin: "I believe it's your generation that will win the cause," she'd said, and she hadn't meant the same "cause" that Tiddy talked about, of making sure the numbers of people alive matched up with the amount of food available. She'd been talking about being free, about getting a government that didn't kill its people, didn't consider third children illegal. And she'd mentioned kids joining the Population Police to fight it from the inside. . . .

Matthias wished fervently that he hadn't dozed off during Mrs. Talbot's story.

As Matthias watched, Nina scooped up cup after cup of fruit. She seemed to be talking to some of the Population Police officers who came through the line. Maybe even flirting.

Would she do that if she were an undercover agent? Matthias wondered.

Wondering about Nina made Matthias's head ache. He spooned soup up to his mouth and bit off hunks of his rolls, but he barely tasted any of it.

Then, just as he was scraping the bottom of his soup bowl, Nina walked out from behind the serving counter. She carried a dishrag in her hand and began casually wiping the tables where people had already finished eating. Matthias's heart started pounding. Should he move over toward one of the tables where she was working?

She came to him instead.

"Act like you don't know me," she whispered, pushing the dishcloth around on a section of table near him. "Don't even look at me."

Matthias peered down into his soup bowl and said nothing. Out of the corner of his eye, he could see Nina pretending to scrub and scrub at some nonexistent stain on the table. She had her back toward the rest of the cafeteria, so no one else could see her talking.

"Go into the front bathroom at seven o'clock tonight. Lock the door."

"Front bathroom? Where's that?" Matthias couldn't help asking. But he had his head bent over, pretending to drink milk from a straw, so he didn't think anyone would notice.

"It's the one closest to the front door," Nina said. "It has silver wallpaper."

And then she moved on to another table.

CHAPTER NINETEEN

Matthias might have sat there all day staring after Nina—or, rather, staring after her while pretending to only be staring off into space. But a few minutes later, an officer in a black uniform pulled up a chair across from him.

"You done eating yet, kid?" the officer asked. "Tiddy told me to watch over you while he's away. I'm Mike."

"Uh, hi," Matthias said. "I was, um, just finishing up." He took the last bite of fruit cocktail and studied Mike while he chewed. Mike was younger and thinner than Tiddy, but he had a similarly friendly manner.

How come none of the Population Police I saw before today ever seemed friendly? Matthias wondered.

He'd never saved a Population Police officer's life before today. He'd never worn a Population Police uniform himself before today.

"We've got an action-packed afternoon ahead of us," Mike said.

Mike's "action" turned out to be mostly a tour of the headquarters and its grounds, but that did, indeed, take hours. Headquarters was a massive building, four stories high and spread out over what seemed to be several acres. The grounds around it seemed more extensive than the city Matthias had grown up in.

"This used to be where some rich guy lived, until the Population Police took over. Can you believe it?" Mike asked as they putt-putted around the property on a golf cart. He got a wistful look on his face. "They say when we get rid of all the rebels—well, not that we're supposed to admit there are rebels, but *you* know—they say when there's peace, all the top Population Police officers will get houses like this, all their own."

"Really?" Matthias said, thinking, *How do you mean, "get rid of all the rebels"? What about children staying with rebels?*

"Has Tiddy left for the, uh, dangerous sectors yet?" he asked anxiously.

Mike misunderstood Matthias's anxiety.

"Don't worry about Tiddy," he said. "That guy always comes out on top." Mike shook his head admiringly.

Matthias wanted to say, *No, no, it's the rebels I'm worried about. What's going to happen to them?* But *was* he just concerned about the rebels? It seemed strange to save somebody's life, then root against him in a battle. Why had he saved Tiddy's life, anyway? Looking back, Matthias had trouble understanding why he'd stopped the shootout by rescuing a Population Police officer. Why hadn't

Matthias just hopped in the car and driven away alone, leaving Tiddy out in the open? Helping the man in the tree to kill him?

Tiddy would have just gone in the cabin to hide. And then Mrs. Talbot would have been in even greater danger.

But it was more than that. It had to do with Samuel telling him, over and over again, "Killing is wrong." Even in the split second he'd had to make a decision back by the cabin, Matthias hadn't wanted to be an accomplice to any more murder. As much as he hated the Population Police, it had bothered him to see the three officers with Tiddy fall down dead.

"Love your enemies," Samuel had also said.

So was it okay that Matthias wanted Tiddy *and* the rebels to survive?

Matthias closed his eyes wearily, too confused and worried to fake interest in formal gardens anymore.

"Getting tired?" Mike said sympathetically. "You've probably seen enough for one day. We'll just go back and get you signed up for the classes Tiddy says you need to take." He drove the golf cart back to the main building, dead leaves crunching under the tires.

Signing up for classes turned out to be a long, drawn-out affair.

"We don't have any record in our files of a Roger Symmes," the woman behind the counter in the training room told Mike.

"Just a minute," Mike told her. He drew Matthias over

to the side and asked, "Tiddy took your I.D. card when he inducted you into the Population Police, didn't he?"

"Uh, no," Matthias said.

Mike rolled his eyes. "That Tiddy. Great guy, of course, but he plays fast and loose with the rules. Can I have your I.D. now?"

Matthias had to dig down deep into his inner pocket to find the card. He handed it over to Mike a little nervously. When he'd taken it from the safe back in the cabin, he'd never pictured having to hand it over to a Population Police officer right in the midst of Population Police headquarters.

But Mike barely glanced at the card.

"I.D. pictures never do anyone justice, do they?" he asked, then carried it over to the woman at the counter.

Matthias couldn't even remember what the picture looked like. But he knew his birthday had just become January 2, his eyes had just become green when they were really more hazel, and his hometown had just become Terpsiko, a place he'd never been to and wouldn't be able to find on a map if his life depended on it. Which it might, someday.

Better look that one up, he told himself.

Mike came back from the counter.

"Okay, you're signed up for gun classes, stealth methods, undercover operations, and subduing enemies," Mike said. "Everything starts tomorrow."

Matthias was so tired and worried and overwhelmed,

he almost missed noticing the irony of the Population Police teaching him to operate undercover.

But of course he couldn't laugh without giving himself away.

CHAPTER *TWENTY*

Mike took Matthias back to the cafeteria for dinner, which turned out to be another hugely filling affair. This time, though, Matthias couldn't sit anonymously at the back of the cafeteria. He sat with Mike and a large, rowdy group of Mike's friends. And it seemed like everyone in the room was watching him.

"Why are those women staring at me?" he finally got the courage to ask when there was a break in the group's merriment.

This set everyone to laughing again.

"Don't you know how the ladies love a hero?" Mike asked. "You know Tiddy and his big mouth. Before he left this afternoon, he told everyone in the building how you'd saved him from certain death."

"Oh," Matthias said.

"Wish Tiddy'd spread some stories about me," one of the others said wistfully. He was a gaunt-faced boy with a crooked nose and a bad case of acne. He winked at the group of women, but they all turned away, making faces as if they'd smelled something horrid.

Mike and his friends laughed harder.

Matthias sat in the midst of all that hubbub feeling as if he'd been transported into an alien world. The bright, warm room full of delicious smells, abundant food, and riffs of laughter didn't seem real. Not when all the laughing people worked for an agency trying to kill children. Not when Percy and Alia were still out there somewhere in the dark, cold night, probably still in pain.

That is, if they were still alive at all.

They're alive, he told himself fiercely. *They've got to be.*

Out of the corner of his eye, he saw Nina walk away from the serving counter across the room. The clock on the wall said six forty-five. He shoveled in the last few bites of his noodle casserole and stood up on legs so sore and tired, they barely held him.

"Hey, kid, you going over to introduce yourself to the ladies?" Mike teased.

"No, just to the bathroom," Matthias said. "Then I'm going to bed," he added, in case it took a long time with Nina. He didn't want Mike and the others to become suspicious or to come in search of him.

The group whistled and made more wisecracks that Matthias didn't catch.

Matthias had to trace his way through twisty hallways to get to the silver bathroom Nina had described. Guards peered at him from nearly every doorway, but none of them stopped him. They all seemed to know who he was.

And they'll all remember seeing me come this way, Matthias thought anxiously, but there was nothing he could do about it.

He reached the bathroom a little early, stepped inside, and locked the door as Nina had instructed. That confused him—how was she supposed to get in if the door was locked? Was he supposed to open the door if he heard knocking? Would she dare to call out to him?

A few seconds later, Matthias understood. Nina came crawling out of a heat vent over the toilet.

"Not my favorite way to get around, but this is a good way to keep our movements secret," Nina muttered as she climbed down over the toilet. She brushed dust from her brown braids and her uniform. "Plus, Trey is so proud of himself for discovering the heat duct system, we use it sometimes just to humor him."

Trey was another of their friends. Matthias felt his heart jump a little at the news that he had another ally at Population Police headquarters.

The bathroom was so tiny that Nina had to stand practically on top of Matthias. She surprised him by seizing him in her arms and giving him a big hug in greeting.

"It's so good to see you, Matthias," Nina whispered. "You'll be so much help here. Where are Percy and Alia stationed? I haven't seen them yet. When did you all join up? It'd be so nice to have Alia in the kitchen with me. . . ."

"Percy and Alia didn't join with me," Matthias whispered

back. "I don't know where they are." Getting those words past the lump in his throat felt like swallowing stones.

"But how—?" Nina asked.

As quickly as he could, Matthias told Nina everything that had happened since the Population Police arrived at Niedler School. By the end, Nina had tears glistening in her eyes.

"Oh, Matthias, I'm so sorry," she murmured.

"So can you and Trey and whoever else is here smuggle me out so I can go back and find them?" Matthias finished up in a rush. His hopes brimmed over.

But Nina frowned, the troubled look deepening in her eyes.

"Matthias, I don't know how we could do that. This place is like a fortress. Just arranging to meet you here in the bathroom was like planning an invasion. They watch me in the kitchen—they watch everyone. And there are so many guards. . . ."

Matthias was so overwhelmed with disappointment, he could barely focus on Nina's words.

"Do you have a plan?" she asked. "Do you know a way out? You and Percy and Alia were so good at getting us out of that Population Police prison."

"That was Percy and Alia," Matthias said bitterly. "They're the clever ones."

He sank down to the floor in despair. Nina bent over and huddled beside him.

"I'll try to think of something," she said. "You try too. And keep your eyes open." She bit her lip. "When we all joined up, we had so many ideas. We were going to tear the Population Police apart from inside. But it's been so hard. . . . None of us could pick where they assigned us. All of us got such menial jobs. Trey scrubs out the garage when the Population Police mechanics are done working on their cars. I'm in the kitchen. Lee—remember Lee?—he shovels out the stall where the top officers have their own horses."

"Trey could cut the brake lines on the Population Police cars," Matthias said. "Lee could make sure the horses buck everybody off. You could put poison in the food."

Matthias felt evil just making those suggestions. *Love your enemies* and *Killing is wrong* echoed in his ears as if Samuel were right there crowded into that tiny room with him and Nina. Matthias was a little relieved when Nina shook her head sadly.

"How could we do any of those things without becoming as bad as the Population Police ourselves?" she asked. "Killing indiscriminately, not caring who dies? And what if we're caught?"

That word—"caught"—seemed to linger in the air, dangerously.

"So you're not doing anything?" Matthias asked.

"We are," Nina said carefully. "I can't tell you what it is. I don't know everything myself. It's . . . Mr. Talbot told us that's the best way to run something like this, so if any of us are caught and interrogated and . . . and tortured, we won't give away everything." She grimaced. "I shouldn't have even mentioned Trey and Lee. Try to forget what I said about them."

Matthias buried his head in his hands. He didn't care about Nina's secrets. He'd pinned such hopes on this meeting with Nina, but it was worthless. He'd just wasted the entire afternoon, when he could have been finding his way back to his friends.

"Matthias?" Nina was saying. "There are stories floating around about you. People say you saved Officer Tidwell's life."

"I did," Matthias said. "Sort of."

"And you went in with Officer Tidwell to a meeting with the commander."

"Yeah," Matthias said.

"But *nobody* sees the commander. Only the other leaders like Officer Tidwell."

"So?" Matthias asked.

"So you've already gotten better access than any of the rest of us, and we've all been here for weeks. I know you want to get back to Percy and Alia but . . . maybe you should let someone else sneak out and go help our friends. Or maybe they're just fine now, with Mrs. Talbot and the guy you saw in the tree."

Matthias looked up at Nina, and it was awful, what she was saying. How could he stay here, helping Nina, never knowing what had happened to Percy and Alia?

Someone began pounding on the bathroom door. Nina scrambled up and struggled to jam herself back through the heat vent.

"Just a minute," Matthias called.

He ran water in the sink, hoping that would mask the sound of the vent cover clanging against the wall. As soon as Nina was out of sight, he opened the door.

Tiddy was standing there, beaming.

"Hey, little buddy, I made it back safely. Aren't you glad?"

"Sure," Matthias said.

"Mike said you worried about me all day," Tiddy continued. "The guards told me you were in here. Mike took good care of you while I was away, didn't he?"

"Uh, yeah," Matthias said. He swallowed hard. "Did you—did you, um, take care of all the bad guys?"

"I'd say so!" Tiddy laughed.

Matthias felt a chill traveling through his body. A premonition of horror.

"How?" Matthias asked. "Did you shoot them all? Forty rebels?" *Don't say you shot any children,* he prayed. *Oh, please, not Percy and Alia.*

"No," Tiddy said regretfully. "None of those cowards dared to show their faces. But we made sure we wouldn't have any more trouble from that sector. We burned them out."

For the first time, Matthias noticed the smudges of ash on Tiddy's face, the tiny, singed hairs escaping from his cap.

"Burned them out?" Matthias repeated stupidly.

"We burned everything within a fifty-mile radius of that cabin," Tiddy said. "Nobody could have survived that!"

CHAPTER *TWENTY-ONE*

Nobody could have survived that. . . . Nobody could have survived that. . . . The words seemed to whirl around Matthias, blocking out every other sound. Maybe Tiddy kept talking; maybe he just stood there waiting for Matthias to congratulate him.

Percy, Matthias thought. *Alia. Mrs. Talbot. The man in the tree. Nobody.*

There was no room for any hope now. No reason to try to move heaven and earth to get back to a certain cabin in a certain woods, the last place he'd seen his friends. The cabin was gone, the woods were gone.

His friends were gone.

Matthias gripped the doorframe because his legs seemed incapable of holding him up now. Matthias was surprised to find his hand could still hold on when his legs had failed: He wouldn't have thought it mattered if he stood or fell. He didn't care anymore if the Population

MARGARET PETERSON HADDIX

Police found him out, learned of his true loyalties. He didn't care if they killed him.

Still, his hand held on.

"—so strange?" Tiddy was asking, and the words seemed to come at Matthias from across a great distance. They seemed to have traveled across a burning woods.

Matthias shrugged, because nothing mattered anymore. But his ears started working again. Tiddy repeated his question. It wasn't, *Why are you acting so strange?* It was, "Why do I feel so strange?"

"Tiddy?" Matthias said cautiously. He was surprised his voice worked. It came out thin and weak, like the birdcalls he and Percy and Alia had used as signals. Not *Whip-poor-will! Whip-poor-will!"* but *What's wrong with Tiddy? What's wrong with Tiddy?*

Tiddy was swaying back and forth, stumbling from side to side.

"My eyes—," he moaned. "I can't see!"

He balled up his fists and rubbed them into his eye sockets. He seemed to be trying to rub his eyes out.

"Don't! Stop!" he screamed.

He fell to the ground and thrashed around as if struggling with an invisible opponent. A few guards standing nearby came over and watched curiously.

"Hey, Tids, what's wrong?" the one asked.

The other yelled out, "Call a medic!"

"I—can't—breathe!" Tiddy gasped.

He clutched his throat and thrashed about even more violently.

And then he stopped moving. His hands loosened from his own throat. His head fell back against the marble floor.

And Matthias knew that Tiddy was dead.

MARGARET PETERSON HADDIX

CHAPTER *TWENTY-TWO*

Matthias went numb. Too much had happened, and nothing made sense. He'd witnessed too many deaths to have any feelings left.

He stood still, clutching the bathroom doorframe while guards ran around, roping off the area by Tiddy's body. Tiddy lay right between two marble pillars, so they had something to tie the ropes to.

"What if it's biological?" someone asked, and then the words "germ warfare" whispered their way through the crowd that had gathered. People began panicking then; they ran.

Matthias kept clutching his doorframe.

The next group of people who came all wore masks over their faces and rubber gloves on their hands. They picked up Tiddy's body. They swabbed the floor with strong-smelling chemicals.

The word they whispered was "poison."

I told Nina she should put poison in the food, Matthias

remembered. *What if she was the one who killed Tiddy?*

The thought didn't lead anywhere. It just fell into the huge pool of Matthias's sorrow and grief and guilt. *Would Tiddy's death be my fault, then, too?* he thought.

One of the masked men came over to Matthias. He peeled Matthias's fingers away from the doorframe.

"Come," he said.

It was the commander. His eyes were wet. He led Matthias by the hand, up the grand staircase, down the twisty halls. He tucked Matthias into a bed in a small room. He gave Matthias something to drink.

"Sleep," he said.

The world flickered out.

When Matthias came back to consciousness, it was daylight again, and the commander was sitting beside Matthias's bed.

"He was like a son to me," the commander said, and Matthias knew he meant Tiddy. "I always had to . . . try not to show it."

The commander stared into Matthias's eyes. Matthias had the feeling that the commander had been there all night, waiting.

"You saved him once," the commander said. "I did not thank you enough for that."

The weight of Matthias's bedding pressed down on him. He felt entombed.

"The scientists figured out what killed him," the commander said. "He'd confiscated some fake identity cards.

They were coated with poison. Slow-acting poison, so the miscreants had time to get away. So Tiddy's friends got to witness his death." The commander was whispering now, each syllable like a dagger of pain. "I—never—should—have—sent—him—back—out—there."

He lowered his head and began sobbing.

So Nina had nothing to do with Tiddy's death, Matthias thought. *Unless the poison I.D. cards were part of the secret project Nina wouldn't tell me about.*

Matthias couldn't find it within himself to care one way or another. Not when Percy and Alia were already dead.

He felt the tears start in his own eyes. Wailing, the commander grasped Matthias's hand and buried his face in Matthias's blanket, and the two of them sobbed their hearts out together—the Population Police commander and the illegal boy. Both, in their own way, abandoned.

CHAPTER *TWENTY-THREE*

The weeks that followed were the strangest of Matthias's life. He stayed in the little bedroom just off the commander's office. He spent hours just staring up at the ceiling, thinking nothing. Nobody mentioned the classes he was supposed to be taking, the duties he might carry out.

The commander came in and out of the room and stroked Matthias's hair from his face. When the hollows deepened in Matthias's face, the commander was the one who ordered that someone come in and feed Matthias three times a day. He was the one who ordered a servant to bathe Matthias every morning, to give him clean clothes.

Matthias wouldn't let anyone wash or throw away the sweater he'd been wearing when he'd arrived at Population Police headquarters.

"It's sentimental for him," he heard the commander tell a particularly determined servant. "Because of Tiddy. Leave it alone."

MARGARET PETERSON HADDIX

Matthias didn't bother correcting the commander. He didn't see any reason to bother doing much of anything. But in spite of himself, his mind swirled with memories. He remembered telling Mrs. Talbot about Samuel's philosophy of life: "Governments will rise and governments will fall, and man will do evil to man, and all we can do is turn our hearts to good."

Matthias couldn't see anymore how Samuel had reached that conclusion.

Don't you know how hard I tried to do good? he thought, wishing he could fling those words at Samuel, at God. But he couldn't feel sure anymore that God listened. *I tried to save Percy and Alia on the Population Police truck, and innocent children died. I tried to take Alia to safety, and Percy got shot. I ran for help and lured Mrs. Talbot to the cabin, and now she's probably dead too, killed in the fire with Percy and Alia and the man in the tree. I saved Tiddy's life, only to watch him die hours later. What does any of it matter?*

He could hear the drone of voices from the commander's office. They were planning something, probably plotting more deaths. Revenge.

So what? Matthias thought. *I tried to do good and ended up killing people. How am I any less evil than the Population Police?*

Once, Nina was the servant who came upstairs with the trayful of food. She tried to talk to him. Matthias grabbed a pad of paper and scribbled out, *NO! Room is bugged!*

He didn't know if it was or not, but it was too painful for him to see the hope in her eyes.

Then let's write back and forth, Nina scribbled back on his pad. *You can help—*

Matthias tore the page off the notepad, tore it to bits. He shook his head violently.

"They're dead," he said aloud. "Don't you understand?"

Nina looked around fearfully. Matthias strode over to the door to the commander's office.

"Sir," he said, "can you send this servant girl away? She's annoying me."

The commander looked coldly at Nina. "Dismissed," he said.

Nina scurried out of the room.

That night the commander came into Matthias's room and sat by his bed.

"People don't understand," he said. "After a loss like we suffered . . ."

"No," Matthias said. "Nobody understands."

"You understand me. I understand you," the commander said.

They sat in companionable silence for a while.

"Tiddy was like a shooting star," the commander finally said. "His zest for life was so great."

A thought flickered in Matthias's mind: *Tiddy was a Population Police officer. His job was killing people. How did that show a zest for life?* But it was followed by the words, *So what? Who cares? Didn't I kill people too?*

"We were working on a plan. It was brilliant, the best ever. Now it's almost ready. And Tiddy's not here to share in the glory with me," the commander said. He stared at Matthias, his red-rimmed eyes burning. "Come on. I want to show you something."

Matthias obediently slid out from under his covers and pulled on slippers that had somehow appeared beside his bed. Matthias had never owned a pair of slippers before in his life.

"No, real clothes," the commander said. "We have to drive somewhere."

He waited while Matthias located his uniform shirt and pants. Amazingly, the pant legs and sleeves didn't have to be rolled up so many times; the belt didn't need to be pulled over to the extra hole. Somehow Matthias had filled out and gotten taller while he was lying around being fed and pampered, in mourning. It seemed like another bit of evil on Matthias's part, that he could keep growing after Percy and Alia were dead.

"Perfect," the commander proclaimed when Matthias was dressed, the starched uniform stiff against his skin.

They stepped out into the hallway. Guards snapped salute after salute as they passed by.

"Someday they'll be saluting you like that," the commander said. "Would you like that?"

They stepped out into the night, and Matthias was startled by the frostiness in the air. Hard-core winter had arrived while he'd been grieving.

"Don't worry. They'll have the car heated for us," the commander said as Matthias shivered.

A car slipped through the darkness and stopped in front of Matthias and the commander. The commander held the door for Matthias, then leaned in and told the driver, "I won't be needing your services tonight. I'll drive myself."

"As you wish, sir," the driver said, and stepped out of the car. "Will you be wanting security behind you?"

"I don't wish to be followed," the commander said sharply. "Is that clear?"

Matthias's heart ached a little as they drove out of the gates. If only he'd left Population Police headquarters weeks ago, the same day he arrived, when there was still time to rescue Percy and Alia.

The world was quiet outside the commander's car. They drove down city streets full of rubble and burned-out buildings. Matthias saw no signs of life in the ruins. He almost could have believed that everyone outside Population Police headquarters was dead.

"The rebellions are over now," the commander said. Matthias gave him a quick glance, and he chuckled. "Oh, yes, *I'm* allowed to admit that there were rebellions. The Population Police had a harder time consolidating power than we expected. But starving people do not make good warriors. And the weather was on our side. Who can fight on an empty belly in the wintertime?"

The commander pulled the car into a dark alley and turned off the engine.

"Quickly," the commander said.

He stepped out of the car, and Matthias followed him, close at his heels. The commander climbed stairs to a brick wall and stabbed a gloved finger at a button Matthias could barely see.

"Glorious future," the commander said into an intercom.

There was a buzzing, and the commander opened a windowless door in the wall. A guard stood just inside the door.

"Commander," he said, managing a flustered salute. "I wasn't expecting you—usually nobody comes at night."

The commander slapped him so hard, the guard's head slammed back against the wall.

"You must be on alert always!" the commander snapped.

The guard said nothing, only bowed his head as if he'd fully deserved the slap, fully deserved the pain.

The commander began walking angrily down a long, vacant corridor. Matthias practically had to run to keep up. When they reached a door on the left side of the corridor, the commander slid a key from his pocket. He looked down at the key, smiling, his anger gone. Then, almost reverently, he slid the key into the lock and turned the doorknob.

Even before the commander flipped on the lights, Matthias had the sense that he was standing before an enormous room. The darkness was that vast. When the lights flickered to life a second later, Matthias could only gape.

In front of him lay a gigantic storeroom of food. Shelves filled with canned goods ran from the floor to the ceiling—and the ceiling was high overhead, seemingly as distant as the sky. Crates of apples, oranges, peaches, and potatoes were stacked as far as the eye could see. Cans of condensed milk and wheels of cheese towered above Matthias's head.

To Matthias, who'd lived on crusts of bread from other people's garbage for most of his life, the sight before him was more dazzling than a roomful of diamonds.

"Ooooh," Matthias breathed out. He wished fervently that Percy and Alia were still alive to see this marvel, to share this view with him. "How did you find all this?"

He was thinking that the Population Police must have caught some amazingly skillful smuggler.

"We didn't 'find' it," the commander replied with a chuckle. "Oh, no. We've been storing up food here for more than a decade. Since the droughts began. Of course, we've had to throw some food away as it rots."

"Throw it away?" Matthias repeated, uncomprehendingly. He looked back and forth between the commander and the mountains of food. When he peered closely, he could see signs of rot on some of the potatoes, bruises on some of the apples, the beginnings of mold on some of the cheese. "You just throw it out?" he said. "But . . . people are starving."

The commander shrugged.

"It's our food, not theirs," he said.

And something happened to Matthias in that moment,

watching the commander shrug. He lost none of his grief, none of his anguish over his friends. But something changed inside him. He looked at the piles of food again, and it was like he was seeing it with new eyes.

This is wrong, he thought. *Letting food rot while people die of hunger. It's evil.*

He thought about all the awful things that had happened that he felt responsible for. The tree falling, killing innocent children, and hurting Alia. Percy being shot. Mrs. Talbot being trapped. He'd never intended anything bad to happen. He'd been trying his hardest to keep everyone safe.

But the Population Police did their evil deeds *deliberately.* The commander knew that people were dying, and he didn't care.

I am not like the commander, Matthias thought. *We have nothing in common.*

An ache grew in his throat and he wanted to sob, but he set his jaw and held it in. He'd been wrong to send Nina away, wrong to refuse to help her, wrong to let the commander treat him like a pet. He'd been wrong to think that everything ended when he lost Percy and Alia.

But those are mistakes I can fix, Matthias told himself. He breathed in the too-sweet smell of rotting food, and it was almost intoxicating. Empowering.

I can stop this evil, he thought.

CHAPTER *TWENTY-FOUR*

It was so hard, walking out of the warehouse, not to recoil from the commander's every touch. The commander put his hand on Matthias's shoulder, and Matthias had to constantly remind himself, *Don't pull away, don't pull away; he has to think you're still on his side.*

The commander slapped the guard again on the way out the door, and it was all Matthias could do not to yell at the commander, *You're just a big bully! You know that?* and to the guard, *Why do you let him do that to you? Why don't you hit him back?*

The commander kicked away a pile of rubbish that had apparently blown up against the car. It turned out not to be rubbish. It was a person, a vagrant who'd curled up against the warmth of the car to sleep. He huddled on the ground in pain—all skin and bones and rags.

And a soul, Matthias told himself, thinking like Samuel again.

Matthias looked around, blinking. All the lumps along

MARGARET PETERSON HADDIX

the warehouse wall that looked like garbage—those were people too. Starving people, just the other side of a wall from untold riches of food. It shook Matthias that he hadn't even noticed them before.

I can make up for that, Matthias thought. *I can beat up the commander, I can lead a charge of the hungry against the door. We can overpower the guard. . . .*

No, he couldn't. As the commander had said, starving people didn't make good warriors. They wouldn't be able to overpower a flea, let alone a well-fed guard. And Matthias, even after growing and filling out, was still just a boy.

With Nina's help, with Trey . . . , Matthias thought, straining to come up with a plan.

"Come along," the commander said.

Matthias got into the car, and the commander tucked a thick blanket around his legs. Matthias realized, as he hadn't before, that the car was familiar: It was Mrs. Talbot's car, the car he and Tiddy had stolen, now restored to its former splendor. Matthias had been too numb to notice before, and now he didn't have time to think about it. They were driving away. Matthias forced himself to pay close attention to the turns they made. *Left at the broken lamppost, right at the sign that says "Wa— hous- Way"* . . . As soon as Matthias got back to his room, he'd write it all down and reverse it, so he could lead Nina and Trey back.

They reached a stretch where the commander didn't

make any turns at all. The commander was humming. Matthias couldn't stand it.

"Why?" he burst out. "Why keep that food, why guard it, if no one's ever going to eat it?"

The commander chuckled.

"Oh, it will be eaten, all right," he said. "In fact, it will serve its purpose very soon."

Matthias tried to keep silent. If he didn't act overly interested, he thought the commander was more likely to talk. But the commander went back to humming.

"What are you going to do with it? How soon?" Matthias asked. He tried to sound overawed and maybe a little bit stupid. How had he sounded before they went into the warehouse, before everything changed?

The commander glanced over at Matthias. His eyes glittered in the darkness. Did he suspect anything?

"Oh, never mind," the commander said. "It's complicated. And it was . . . it was Tiddy's plan."

"Tiddy," Matthias echoed sadly. He was totally acting now, playing the word for effect.

He looked over, and the commander had tears streaming down his face.

And, in spite of himself, Matthias felt guilty.

CHAPTER TWENTY-FIVE

Matthias got up the next morning and dressed himself. When a servant brought a tray of food into his room, he announced, "I won't be needing that anymore. From now on, I'll be eating down in the cafeteria with everyone else."

"But, sir," the servant said, "what shall I do with all this food?"

Matthias considered. The main part of the meal was eggs scrambled with cheese—a total luxury. The tray also held a plateful of toast, a bowl of cooked apple slices, and a frothing glass of milk.

"Eat it yourself," he decided.

"Oh, sir," the servant said. "Can I?"

She was a pock-faced girl as scrawny as Matthias had been when he'd first arrived at Population Police headquarters. Matthias supposed she spent her days carrying around food that she herself was not allowed to eat.

"Go right ahead," Matthias said. "But—don't tell anyone."

"Oh, no, I won't," the girl said, curtsying. "Thank you, sir."

Matthias walked out of his room through the commander's office. The commander was bent over stacks of papers. Matthias stood close and tried to look at the papers without appearing interested, but the numbers marching across the pages meant nothing to him.

"Sir," Matthias said, "I've been thinking. I don't believe . . . Tiddy . . . would want me to just lie around all the time, grieving. I need to . . . do something. In his memory."

Matthias wasn't really lying. It was just that he'd be acting in honor of Percy's and Alia's memory, and Samuel's and Mrs. Talbot's. Not Tiddy's.

The commander reached out and ruffled Matthias's hair.

"You're a brave boy," he muttered sadly.

Matthias climbed down the stairs feeling anything but brave. He walked into the cafeteria, and the entire room became instantly hushed. Matthias felt like every eye in the room was on him.

How am I supposed to carry out a secret plan with everyone watching? Matthias wondered.

He made himself stumble on over to the woman with the trays.

"I don't know—am I supposed to hand you money or a voucher or something?" he asked her. "Last time Mike took care of me, and before that, Tiddy."

"Oh, you're that boy of Tiddy's," the woman crooned softly. "Oh, you poor dear. Now, don't you worry about anything. Just go on and eat."

"Thank you," Matthias mumbled.

When he stepped over to the women doling out the food, he was overjoyed to see Nina's familiar brown eyes above one of the face masks. He quickly slid his hand in and out of his pocket and was ready when she handed him a bowl of oatmeal. His fingertips brushed hers; when they both pulled away, he was holding the bowl and she was holding a coiled-up scrap of paper he'd been carrying around. Her eyes widened a bit with surprise, but otherwise, she gave no indication that anything had passed between them.

Matthias took his tray of food and sat down. He hoped Nina would understand the note he'd written: *Same meeting place. What time?* He ate his oatmeal slowly, lingering over every bite. So he was one of the few diners who remained when Nina came out to scrub the tables. She leaned close to his ear as she stretched to reach the opposite side of his table.

"Fifteen minutes from now," she whispered, and moved on.

Matthias scraped the last flecks of oatmeal out of his bowl, swallowed, and pushed himself away from the table. He had extra time, so he took a roundabout route to the silver bathroom. But he got delayed in the front hall because a huge crowd was gathered there, blocking his way.

"Excuse me," he murmured. "Could you let me through?"

The cluster of dark uniforms around him seemed like a forest, impenetrable. Then one officer glanced down at him.

"It's the boy," she gasped, and the clump of uniforms parted before him.

Matthias walked forward as officers moved aside to give him even more room. This wasn't what he was used to. He was used to having to scramble between people's legs, always having to watch out so nobody stepped on him. He wasn't used to being noticed at all, and now everyone was staring at him, almost reverently.

He reached the front of the crowd. He was facing the very spot where Tiddy had died, the two pillars now framing a huge vase full of roses. A banner across the floral arrangement proclaimed, ONE OF OUR BEST. Around the display of roses, people had left mementos and messages. Matthias saw ribbons and medals, bracelets and scraps of paper covered in heart-broken scrawls: WE MISS YOU, TIDDY.

The crowd was absolutely silent, watching Matthias. He realized they expected him to add something to the memorial, but he'd brought nothing with him; he hadn't even known there *was* a memorial. Thinking frantically, he looked around, and his cap rattled against his ears. The cap! Well, that would have to do. He took off his cap and left it at the base of the roses. Then he backed away, watching the crowd. People began following his example, surging forward to lay their own caps beside Matthias's.

Now everyone was watching the impromptu cap-laying service, so Matthias was able to duck into the silver bathroom without being seen.

His heart pounded strangely. *What was that all about?* he wondered.

He peered into the vent where Nina had climbed out the last time, but the duct beyond was empty and dark.

Someone knocked on the door. "Cleaning!"

It was Nina's voice. Matthias fumbled with the lock, and then she slipped through the doorway.

"Aren't you scared someone might have seen you?" Matthias asked. "There are a hundred people out there."

"Believe me, I'm invisible," Nina said wryly. "And anyone who wants to check will see I've been loaned from the kitchen to the housecleaning crew." She set down a large bucket full of cleaning solutions, scrub brushes, and rags on the floor. She squirted a stream of ammonia into the toilet, selected a brush, and began scrubbing.

Matthias made a face at the overpowering odor. "Do you have to do that while we're talking?" he asked.

"Yes, I do," Nina said. "They time us. If I don't have this bathroom sparkling clean in ten minutes, I'm in trouble."

"I'll do the sink, then," Matthias said.

Nina handed him his own bottle of noxious chemicals.

"Why did you want to meet?" she asked as they both scrubbed away.

Matthias told her about the immense storehouse of food and his idea that it could be distributed to the hungry.

"Hmm," Nina said.

"Hmm? That's all you can say?" Matthias asked. "The Population Police have food, and people are starving. So let's give it away."

"Matthias, it's not that simple," Nina said. "Where is this warehouse again?"

Matthias told her as best he could.

"Oh," Nina said. "That's a problem."

"Why?"

Nina shook her head, her braids thumping against her thin shoulders.

"Never mind," she said. "I shouldn't have said that."

Matthias pushed his rag against the porcelain so hard, he feared he'd pull the sink from the wall.

"It *is* simple," Matthias said. "You and me and Trey, we can work together. It'd be like—" He almost said, *like Percy and Alia and me,* but the words stuck in his throat.

Nina let the brush fall into the toilet. She stared at Matthias, her eyes wide and distressed.

"Matthias, it's just that . . . Trey and—and the others . . . they don't know you like I do. They're a little bit suspicious, because you've had it so easy ever since you got here. The rest of us are being worked to death, and you're getting your food delivered on trays. And people are saying that you're Tiddy's son or maybe the commander's long-lost grandson. And you haven't been acting like you want to help us with—"

"I lost my friends!" Matthias protested, his voice

coming out entirely too loud for someone holding a secret meeting.

"But don't you see?" Nina said, her eyes burning. "We all have—we've either lost someone we loved or left someone behind or been through some terrible experience. Or maybe all of those. But we're going on. That's why we're doing what we're doing, because of what we went through."

"So am I," Matthias muttered. He blinked hard, trying desperately not to break down. Not in front of Nina. Not when she sounded so fierce.

"But what you're telling me now, it's too perfect," Nina said. "It's almost like we're being set up."

Matthias froze. He could feel the harsh chemicals of the cleaning supplies eating into his skin.

"You think I'm lying?" he asked. "Making it all up? I was *there*. I saw the food. I *smelled* it."

His voice was too loud again. Nina winced and glanced anxiously toward the door.

"*I* believe you," she said soothingly, her voice a near whisper. "I know you think you're telling me the truth. But if the commander somehow knew about our plot, if he somehow knew you were connected to us, then the perfect way to ruin our plot would be to set up this fake storehouse of food, get you to tell us about it, and totally distract us from our goal."

Matthias stared at her.

"You think it was fake?" he finally said. "You think I'm being *used*?"

"I don't know what to think," Nina said. "Go back to the commander. Keep acting like—like his grandson or whatever, to make sure he still likes you. And spy on him. Eavesdrop on his meetings. Steal papers from his desk. Find out what *his* plan for all that food is. Just . . ."

Nina reached out and very gently touched Matthias's cheek.

"Just what?" Matthias asked.

"Just don't get caught."

CHAPTER TWENTY-SIX

Matthias walked back to his bedroom in a daze, his hands reeking of ammonia. He started to walk in through the commander's office, then stopped.

"There's another door, isn't there?" he asked the guard. "I have to get something from my room, and I don't want to . . . disturb the commander."

"Sure," the guard said. "Over here."

He led Matthias down a short hallway off to the side. The guard unlocked a door, and Matthias stepped into his bedroom.

"Thanks," Matthias said. "Should I lock the door again when I leave?"

"It'll lock automatically behind you," the guard said.

That's useful information, Matthias told himself. *Start paying attention again.*

He walked over to his window and looked out. He was on the second floor, facing a courtyard.

If I need to, I can knot my sheets and climb down. I'll have to find out which of those windows below would be the safest to enter. That way, I can sneak out and nobody will know.

But he could see the shadows of guards standing by the windows below, their dark shapes humped over like vultures. The old despair threatened to overwhelm Matthias again.

It doesn't matter, he told himself. *Right now, I don't need to get out without anyone knowing. I need to eavesdrop on the commander. Might as well start now. Unless the guard talked to the commander, he doesn't even know I'm here. . . .*

Blindly, blinking back tears, Matthias stumbled over to the door separating his bedroom from the commander's office. He pressed his ear tightly against the hard wood. Nothing happened, except that his ear began to hurt. He could hear soft murmurings, but he couldn't make out any words. The door was too thick.

Then he heard footsteps.

He scrambled away from the door and made a half dive for the bed. He was sprawled half on, half off the bed when the door opened. He buried his head in his pillow to hide his guilty expression.

The footsteps came closer.

"Oh, my dear boy." It was the commander. He sat down on the edge of the bed and began stroking Matthias's hair. "It's hard, isn't it?"

Matthias moved his head up and down, burrowing deeper and deeper into the pillow. Yes, this was hard. He shoved his hands under the pillow and hoped the commander wouldn't notice the ammonia smell.

"I don't think you should push yourself too hard," the commander said. "Going down to breakfast and then seeing Tiddy's memorial . . . that's a lot for one morning. Several people have told me what you did. . . . They were all so moved. Do you know how many caps are down there now? Five hundred."

Great, Matthias thought. *Not only do people watch everything I do, they report everything to the commander.*

He wasn't particularly surprised. How else had the commander known Matthias was back in his room?

The despair came creeping back, ready to drown him. Who was he to think he could outsmart the Population Police? How could he and Nina and Trey and Lee—mere children—do anything when the Population Police had all the power? The Population Police had this grand headquarters, storehouses of food, endless numbers of guards and soldiers stretched out across the entire country.

Matthias was choosing to side with starving people dying on the street.

And God. And goodness. And mercy. And hope.

The words came into his mind so strongly that he almost glanced around to see if Samuel or Percy or Alia were standing right there with him, telling him what to think. At the last minute, he remembered who was sitting beside him. Peeking out from his pillow, Matthias could see the commander's stiff black uniform, with the row of commendations along his sleeve. Commendations for killing people, probably, for ordering the deaths of children like Matthias.

How can I not fight back?

Matthias got an idea. He turned his head to the side. He hoped his face was red and anguished-looking enough.

"Tiddy wanted me to . . . take classes," he muttered. "I'm so far behind."

"There'll be plenty of time for that later," the commander said. He patted Matthias's back.

"Could I listen to tapes of the classes?" Matthias asked, trying to make it sound like the idea had just occurred to him. "With headphones, I mean, so I don't disturb you."

"Why, that's a splendid notion," the commander said. "Of course. I'll send for that right away."

When Matthias went downstairs for lunch a few hours later, he had a new note scribbled out to shove into Nina's hand: *Will spy for you. Have headphones. Can you get listening device for me?*

CHAPTER TWENTY-SEVEN

Three days passed before Matthias got any sort of answer to his note. He spent the time figuring out the brand-new headphones and shiny, state-of-the-art tape recorder the commander had given him. All the electronic equipment Matthias had ever used before had been salvaged from trash piles—battered, dented, and just one frayed wire away from not working at all. In fact, none of the equipment had been anything but trash until Percy worked his magic on it, splicing wires, taping cracks.

Matthias wished for just a fraction of Percy's skill. He was going to need it.

When Nina finally palmed a tiny coinlike disk into his hand one night at dinner, he wondered that it came with no directions, no explanations.

"I—," he began.

Nina glared at him.

"That's the best soup we have tonight," she said. "Surely you're not going to complain?"

Matthias got her meaning.

Late that night he sat fiddling with the bug and his tape recorder. The recorder had a radio with it, and if he found the right frequency, he could set the radio to pick up transmissions from the listening device. Couldn't he?

He put the headphones on and began turning the dial of the radio.

"I'm alone," he said aloud, to test the bug. "I miss . . . everybody."

Only static crackled in his headphones.

"I miss you," he said again, turning the dial slowly. "I miss you, I miss you, I miss you. . . ."

His headphones still weren't picking up any sound, but he found the soft litany comforting anyhow. He missed Percy and Alia and Samuel. He missed being an innocent little kid looking up to a wise old man who seemed to know everything. He missed playing games with Percy and Alia and curling up with them at night like a litter of puppies. He missed Samuel's kind eyes and Alia's shy grin and Percy's mussed-up hair falling down into his eyes.

"I miss you," he said again, his voice nearly a sob.

Wait—had the sound come out of his headphones this time?

Just then, his door opened. Matthias quickly slid the bug into his pocket. The motion set off a racket in his headphones. He flipped the switch to turn off his radio.

"Are you all right?" the commander asked, poking his head in the door.

"Uh, fine," Matthias lied. "Just listening to my tapes."

He hoped the commander didn't look too closely. The tape recorder was empty.

"I was afraid you might be lonely," the commander said gently.

"I was thinking about . . . Tiddy," Matthias said. It was such a struggle to keep an innocent expression on his face as he stared back at the commander. Because he understood suddenly: Somehow the commander had heard him saying, "I'm alone . . . I miss you." But he'd been speaking so softly, and if the walls and doors were too thick for Matthias to hear distinct words from the commander's office, then they were too thick for the commander to hear distinct words from Matthias's room.

Unless Matthias's room was bugged, just as he'd angrily suggested to Nina.

Just as he was planning to do to the commander's room.

Matthias's head fell forward, and he buried his face in his hands. He thought maybe he'd given himself away, but when he peeked out through the cracks between his fingers, the commander was still peering at him sympathetically.

The commander thought he was just in despair over Tiddy.

"Do you want to talk about it?" the commander asked, and he did sound like some kindly old grandfather.

Some kindly old grandfather who sends soldiers out to kill innocent children. Some kindly old grandfather who lets food rot while people starve, Matthias thought.

"I . . . can't," Matthias murmured. "You tell me . . . about Tiddy before I met him."

The commander settled into an armchair beside Matthias's bed. He leaned forward, just the way Samuel used to when he told bedtime stories to Matthias, Percy, and Alia. The memory made Matthias ache, and he almost missed the commander's first words.

"Tiddy joined the Population Police when he was just a teenager," the commander said. "Right after the Population Police were formed. Those first few years were . . . chaotic. Some doubted we could ever succeed. But Tiddy was always so optimistic, so eager, so loyal. He was assigned to my detail, and we'd be out making our rounds, looking for criminals, and it'd be tense, stressful work, and Tiddy would be cracking jokes, keeping all of our spirits up. . . ."

Those "criminals," Matthias reminded himself, were children like him. Tiddy had been cracking jokes on the way to killing people.

The commander leaned his head back and stared off dreamily.

"When I was put in charge of our identification program—did you know that's what I do?—I requested that Tiddy be transferred to my unit. Just because I liked him. I never thought he'd come up with the most brilliant plan of all."

Could Matthias get away with asking what the plan was? Would the commander just tell him, flat out, without

Matthias having to eavesdrop at all? Could Matthias believe whatever the commander chose to tell?

Matthias was so busy wondering, he missed his chance. The commander was standing up.

"Here," he said. "I'll show you pictures of Tiddy in the early years."

Matthias slipped out of bed and followed the commander into his office. The commander flipped on his desk light, and it made a small oasis of light in the dark, cavernous room. Matthias shivered and leaned in close, looking over the commander's shoulder. Matthias was near enough to count each individual gray hair springing from the commander's scalp.

I could hurt him, Matthias thought, strangely. *Even kill him. Now, when he's not looking. When he trusts me . . . Would Nina want me to do that?*

Matthias trembled at the thought, at the evilness that seemed to lurk all around him in the dark of the commander's office.

"Are you cold?" the commander asked. "Here."

He got up, went into Matthias's bedroom, and returned with the blanket from Matthias's bed. He tucked it around Matthias's shoulders, then sat back down and pulled an envelope from his desk.

"This is Tiddy at his commissioning ceremony," the commander said, holding out a picture of a very young Tiddy looking very formal. "And afterward," he added. The next photo showed Tiddy in the center of a group of laughing young men, all tossing their caps into the sky. They didn't look like soldiers preparing to go out and kill babies. They looked like young men laughing uproariously, without a single care in the world.

Almost against his will, Matthias drew in closer, hypnotized by each successive photo of the life of Population Police Officer Tidwell. But, while he looked, he angled his right side out of the commander's view. He plunged his hand into his pocket, then groped along the underside of the edge of the commander's desk. A tiny lip of wood jutted out over the base of the desk. Would the bug stick there without being spotted?

Matthias couldn't be sure of anything, but he held the bug behind his back and, under the cover of the blanket, peeled off an adhesive strip. Then he stuck the bug under the desk.

Oh, please, Matthias thought, and it was pretty much his first prayer since witnessing Tiddy's death. But those two small words carried so many hopes: He was praying that the bug would stick, that it'd work, that no one would find it, that he'd hear something that would help him and Nina and Trey.

And maybe he was even praying that the laughing Population Police Officer Tidwell somehow now understood the evil he'd done.

CHAPTER *TWENTY-EIGHT*

Matthias put on his headphones and switched on his radio as soon as he woke up the next morning. At first all he heard was the rustle of papers, presumably as the commander moved them across his desk. He was just ready to give up and go down for breakfast when a sharp voice burst through his headphones: "Commander, my report!"

"Go ahead," the commander said.

"We are ninety-five percent done with Project Exchange," the voice said.

"Very good," the commander said. "When do you anticipate completion of the project?"

"Next week."

"Wonderful," the commander said. "Carry on."

Matthias kept listening, but that was all. He wrote down *Project Exchange 95% done—finish expected next week* on a scrap of paper and handed it to Nina in the cafeteria a few minutes later when she handed him a bowl of Cream of Wheat. He knew what a dangerous thing he was doing. If the bug was found—if he was caught—he'd probably have no chance to pass along stored-up information to Nina. So he'd have to tell her everything as he learned it.

He had nothing new to report by lunchtime, but Nina surprised him by slipping a note into his hand along with a mug of cider.

That's very bad news, the note said, when Matthias had a chance to read it back in his room after lunch. The "very" was underlined six times. *We have to hurry. Keep listening!!!!*

Matthias put his headphones back on immediately, but it was frustrating to sit around straining to hear silence. And it was maddening not to know what Nina, Trey, and the mysterious "others" were hurrying to do.

Samuel, am I doing the right thing? You didn't believe in getting involved in politics. Is this politics? All I want is to get that food to the starving people. What if there's something bad in Nina's plan?

Once, when he'd first met Nina, she had risked her life because she thought that was the only way to save Matthias's—Matthias's and Percy's and Alia's. But just because Nina was trustworthy then, was she still trustworthy now?

God, why isn't life as simple as Samuel always made me think it was?

The headphones crackled to life.

"Sir?" This was a young voice. "Officer Jason Barstow reporting to demonstrate the test for Project Authenticity."

"Of course. Come in." The commander practically purred.

There was a thud, as if something heavy had been placed on the desk.

"Gotta protect your furniture." It was the young voice again—Officer Barstow's.

"I appreciate that," the commander said, an edge of sarcasm in his tone.

"Now, these cards both look absolutely identical, correct? Both absolutely authentic?" Officer Barstow asked.

"Yes," the commander said. Several others must have come in to watch the demonstration with him because an echo came through the headphones: "Yes . . . Yes . . . Yes . . . Yes . . ."

"If you had to guess, which one would you say is fake?" Officer Barstow asked.

A long silence followed. Finally the commander said doubtfully, "This one?"

"Other opinions?" Officer Barstow asked.

Are they looking at I.D. cards? Matthias wondered. *The commander said he was in charge of the identification program. . . .*

The others in the commander's office made their choices quickly.

"Ah, so everyone agrees with the commander," Officer Barstow said. "Let's see."

Matthias heard a sizzling sound, then a string of "ooh's" and "aah's."

"So we were all wrong," the commander said, a steely

tone in his voice. "Try it again on different cards. Ones *I* know are fake or real."

Matthias could picture the commander reaching into his own drawer, throwing down a pile of identity cards on his desk, like a challenge.

More sizzling.

"Yes," the commander said. "That's correct. It works. It works perfectly."

He sounded like he was grinning. A burst of applause roared out of Matthias's headphones so loudly that Matthias had to pull them away from his ears. But he still heard Officer Barstow's final words: "It's absolutely foolproof."

CHAPTER TWENTY-NINE

Matthias's head spun. He took off his headphones, but his ears still rang with the sound of the officials' applause.

Why are they so excited? Matthias wondered. *They've been able to find fake I.D.'s before.* His weeks in Population Police prison proved that.

"Absolutely foolproof," Officer Barstow had said. He'd sounded smug and overwhelmingly happy, like he'd just found enough food to feed everyone or figured out a way to end all disease.

No, Matthias reminded himself. *This is the Population Police. They'd be overjoyed over some absolutely foolproof way to kill third children.*

Third children. Matthias. Nina. Trey. Lee. And all the others.

It wasn't anywhere near dinnertime yet, but Matthias tore out of his room and raced for the cafeteria. The doors were locked, and a guard stood before them, looking bored.

"I'm hungry," Matthias announced. "Think there's any way I could sneak in there and get a snack?"

"Of course n—," the guard started to snap. Then he looked at Matthias more closely. "Oh. You're Tiddy's friend. Sure, go ahead. They'll do anything for you."

The guard opened the doors and Matthias slipped inside.

What if Nina's loaned out to housekeeping detail this afternoon? What will I do then?

But Nina was in the kitchen, chopping carrots alongside several other girls. How was Matthias supposed to get her away to talk to him alone? They should have worked out a code word, he realized. They should have worked out a whole coded language.

And then Matthias knew what to say.

"Excuse me." He tried to sound childish and innocent, like the little kid he'd been back when Samuel was alive. "I saw this really neato, interesting bug outside, and I don't know what it was, and I thought if someone could come look at it with me . . . It's the kind of thing Tiddy could have helped me with."

He saw the girls exchange glances at Tiddy's name.

"A bug?" one of the girls said. "Outdoors? In January?"

Oops, Matthias thought.

But "I'll go with him," Nina said, sighing heavily, like it was a big sacrifice. "I've got to hang out those wet towels anyhow."

"Be quick about it," a hatchet-faced woman said from

behind Nina. "No dawdling over some silly insect that doesn't know enough to die in the wintertime." She punched down a huge lump of bread dough for emphasis.

Nina paused to pick up a big basket of towels, then Matthias followed her out a back door.

"Where's the bug?" she said in a bright, fake voice that was probably mostly for the benefit of the girls and women who might still be able to hear from the kitchen.

"There's one in my room, for starters," Matthias whispered back. "Not the insect kind. That's why I didn't want to meet anywhere inside. What if there's a bug in the bathroom, too?"

"What if there's a bug on your uniform?" Nina countered. "What if there's a bug in that tree?" She pointed up at a stunted, leafless branch overhead. "This is dangerous, us being seen together."

She plopped down her basket of towels before a makeshift clothesline.

"But I had to tell you what I heard," Matthias said. Quickly, he reported on the demonstration in the commander's office. The more Matthias talked, the more terrified Nina looked. Her face went pale and drawn. She dropped the towel she'd started to hang on the line. She gasped just at the mention of Officer Barstow's name.

"Are you sure it was Officer Jason Barstow?" she demanded.

"Yeah," Matthias said.

"But that's my Jason—I mean, the one who tricked me.

It was his fault I ended up in Population Police prison. I'd heard he was involved in some big, secret project for the Population Police, but . . ."

Matthias kept talking. Nina began shaking her head violently when he got to the part about the sizzling sound, the officers' applause.

"No, it can't be true. They can't be ready so soon," she moaned.

"And they've got our I.D. cards," Matthias finished up. "Right? They took mine away when I joined the Population Police—well, a little after that, because Tiddy forgot. Do they have yours and Trey's and everyone else's, too? Do you think they'd use that Project Authenticity test on our cards, even though we're in the Population Police?"

Nina's eyes burned into his.

"Yes," she whispered.

"Then we've got to run away," Matthias said. "Leave the Population Police, go somewhere we can get other fake I.D.'s. . . ."

He didn't know how it was possible. Even from the backyard, standing by Nina's clothesline, he could see the enormous wall, the stern line of Population Police guards by the gate.

Nina was shaking her head anyway.

"Matthias, it doesn't matter if we run away or not," she said sadly. "They're going to do that new test on everybody's I.D. Everybody's in the entire country."

CHAPTER *THIRTY*

Matthias felt no surprise, just a growing sense of dread. The empty tree branches above him clicked together ominously in the cold wind, as if they were counting off the final minutes of his life. His, and so many other children's.

"I think I can tell you this now," Nina said. "It's not really so secret anymore. Remember Project Exchange, that you wrote that note about earlier? The project they're supposed to finish next week? The Population Police ordered everyone in the country to turn in every I.D. card. That's what's been happening the past few weeks while you've been . . ."

"Hanging out with the commander," Matthias finished for her. "Getting my food on trays."

Nina grimaced and nodded.

"People get receipts for their I.D.'s," she said. "The Population Police say they'll get their original I.D.'s back soon. But there have been all sorts of rumors going around about what the Population Police intend to do with all those I.D. cards in between. We heard about Project Authenticity, but we weren't sure . . . we hoped . . . we didn't want to believe it was true. But you just gave me the proof."

"Now they can catch every third child who has a fake I.D.," Matthias said. "And no third child without a fake I.D. will ever dare to come out of hiding."

"Right," Nina said. "It'll be the Population Police's dearest dream come true."

Matthias stared out into the frozen landscape, fighting a sense of hopelessness.

"Why are they going to so much bother?" he asked. "To collect every I.D., from every person in the entire country? Why didn't they wait until they were sure the authenticity test worked, then just go house to house, testing as they went?"

"We think they don't want the word to get out," Nina said. "They want to do everybody's at once, so nobody will know ahead of time what's going to happen."

She bent to pick up a wet towel and flung it over the clothesline. Matthias watched her red, chapped hands fumble with the clothespin.

"But you've got a plan, right?" Matthias asked.

"We did," Nina said glumly. "We've had lots of plans since we got here."

She kept hanging up towels.

"Do you know where the Population Police are keeping

all the I.D.'s?" Matthias asked. "Can't you go and—I don't know—burn down the building or something?"

"We thought of that," Nina said. "We thought it was a brilliant idea. But you put a stop to those plans." She shook her head sorrowfully.

"Me?" Matthias was astonished. "What did I do?"

"You told us where the Population Police keep their extra food."

"So?"

Nina turned to face Matthias, tears glistening in her eyes.

"The food and the I.D.'s—they're all in the same place."

CHAPTER *THIRTY-ONE*

For a moment, Matthias didn't understand. He'd had too much to try to make sense of, going back to Tiddy's death, Percy's and Alia's injuries, Samuel's death. No—going all the way back to his parents abandoning him. He still couldn't make sense of the earliest events of his life. How was he supposed to make sense of this?

"We think the Population Police did it that way on purpose. They must suspect there are saboteurs around who wouldn't strike if they feared destroying the food as well," Nina was saying.

"So the commander was using me, showing me the food," Matthias said, his panic growing. "He must suspect—that's why he bugged my room."

"You can't be sure of that," Nina said. "They have bugs in lots of rooms. The Population Police are bug crazy. Anyhow, after you told me about the warehouse, we heard the same story from other sources."

Matthias shook his head, trying to clear his mind.

"It's just spare food, in that warehouse," he said slowly.

"Maybe," Nina said. "I hear things sometimes, in the kitchen. There was a bad harvest this year—with the Government changing, too many people were out fighting and not enough people were out getting crops from the fields. So that food in the warehouse may be . . . necessary . . . to get our country through the winter."

"*May* be?" Matthias asked.

"How can we know for sure?" Nina said with a hopeless shrug. "And yet—we have to know for sure before we make any decisions. Before we take any action."

The cold seemed to be seeping all the way into Matthias's soul. Or maybe it was just the despair in Nina's voice getting to him.

"Trey says this is irony," Nina said bitterly. "He says that we've got to make the same decision that the Government faced all those years ago, after the droughts and famines. Protect third children and take the chance that other people will starve. Or let the Population Police kill third children and make sure that other people live."

"Isn't there another choice?" Matthias whispered.

"You tell me," Nina said.

Matthias could only stare at her, openmouthed, his breath freezing right before his eyes. After a few moments, Nina whipped the last of the wet towels onto the line and headed back toward the kitchen.

"Come on," she said. "I'm going to get in trouble for staying out here so long."

He blindly stumbled after her. Neither one of them bothered to look at some pretend insect on the ground.

It didn't seem to matter anymore.

CHAPTER *THIRTY-TWO*

Matthias lay on his bed, his face buried in his pillow, his headphones dangling around his neck. Ever since he'd talked to Nina, he'd been having trouble listening to what was going on in the commander's office. Every stray thump might be someone coming in, ready to report on a spy ring in their midst. Or the commander slamming a door, ready to confront Matthias about the bug he found under his desk. Or—

"Stop it," Matthias said aloud. Then he remembered the bug in his own room. "Stop, um, crying over Tiddy," he added, just in case someone was listening. "You're acting like a little boy."

I am acting like a little boy, Matthias thought. *Hiding my head under my pillow, pretending all the bad news will go away if I don't hear it . . .*

Resolutely, he jerked the headphones back over his ears.

"—grand ceremony?" someone was saying.

"Of course it has to be grand!" This was the commander's

voice, roaring out so fiercely that Matthias winced. "We have to make the people remember this forever. All that food is theirs because we, the Population Police, got rid of all the illegals. The people must love us and hate the enemy."

"Okay. So the president will announce the successful completion of Project Authenticity, blah, blah, blah. . . ."

"What kind of speechwriter are you—'blah, blah, blah'?"

"Hey, it'll sound good when he says it. Do you want him to read the names of everyone you dispose of? That kind of thing is always so dramatic."

Dispose of? Matthias thought, shivering. They made it sound like they were just taking out the trash. He couldn't understand their jaunty tones, their high spirits. They were talking about killing people.

Samuel? Matthias wanted to ask his old friend. *Why didn't you tell me that evil could be so lighthearted?*

Somehow that made it even more frightening.

"We have some issues to consider if he reads the names," the commander said, and he at least sounded serious. "Do we read the traitors' names, too?"

"Sure, why not? The more the merrier."

Matthias fought to hold in a gasp.

Someone cleared his throat, and Matthias had the feeling that it was the commander.

"It may seem that we are governing sheep who will believe and obey anything we tell them," the commander said. "But may I remind you that as recently as two months ago, one of those 'sheep' passed a poisoned I.D. card to one of our best officers."

The mention of Tiddy's death seemed to silence the more jovial Population Police officers. The commander continued.

"Even our most gullible subject will have trouble believing that—let's see"—the commander ruffled some papers and seemed to be reading aloud—"that 'Reginald Henry, age thirty-five' is an illegal third child."

Matthias didn't know how long the Population Law had been in effect, but he was pretty sure the oldest illegal third children were still teenagers. What was the commander talking about?

"Then we just won't announce the traitors' names," someone said carelessly. Matthias thought it might be the speechwriter again. "Or announce them separately from Project Authenticity."

"It's just so convenient to have everything under the Project Authenticity umbrella," the commander mused. "You have a fake I.D., you're the enemy, you die."

"Or you have a legitimate I.D., but we say the authenticity test came up negative," someone else said with a chuckle. "Because you're just not one of our best friends."

"All our enemies gone in one fell swoop," the commander said dreamily.

"And the people rewarded with a grand ceremony."

"A festival!"

"A feast!"

Matthias realized he'd clapped his hands over his ears. He barely stopped himself from ripping his headphones off and throwing them across the room. He thought he understood the Population Police plan now. They were going to use Project Authenticity as an excuse to weed out all their enemies: all the third children, all the people who were working undercover with fake I.D.'s, all the people who had ever opposed the Population Police. And then, when all the opposition was dead, the Population Police would bring out the food from the warehouse. And the ordinary people would think they were getting it because the bad guys were gone.

That was why the food and the I.D.'s were stored together.

"Evil," Matthias muttered. "Evil, evil, evil."

He understood now how happy Samuel must have felt to finally stand up, right in front of the Population Police, and shout out, "What you are doing is wrong!" What a relief that must have been, even though it had led to his death.

Matthias wanted to storm into the commander's office right now and shout out, *You're evil!* It wouldn't do any good, but they were going to kill him anyway, as soon as they found out he wasn't really Roger Symmes.

Why not go out shouting? Matthias thought.

Because Nina was downstairs in the kitchen waiting for Matthias's reports on the commander's conversations.

Because Matthias coming clean might also endanger Nina and Trey and the mysterious "others."

Because there was still a chance . . .

Matthias felt like he'd been in danger of plunging over some huge cliff and had just barely managed to step back from the edge. He forced himself to listen to the headphones again. He'd missed hearing what the decision was about reading the traitors' names. The officers seemed to be wrapping up their meeting.

"So the ceremony will be next Friday," the speechwriter was saying. "I'll have the president's speech ready."

"And I think the Power Commission will be able to work a little miracle of its own—we'll have all the electricity back in service by then, so the entire country will be able to see the ceremony on TV," someone else said.

"Perfect," the commander said. "Food distribution will begin Friday night."

If only all the TVs worked before next Friday, Matthias thought. *If only we could use them to get the word out about the food before they start running Project Authenticity. If only we could tell the whole country the truth about what's going on. If only we could warn all the third children, all the rebels. If only we could just hand out all that food now. . . .*

Matthias bolted upright on his bed, jerking up so quickly that he yanked the headphone cord out of the tape recorder. He didn't know how to accomplish all of those "if only's."

But one of them just might be possible.

CHAPTER THIRTY-THREE

Nina saw plenty of holes in Matthias's plan, but she didn't shoot it down entirely.

"Maybe we can work with that," she said thoughtfully.

They were hiding in a walk-in freezer at the back of the giant kitchen. It was the middle of the night, and Matthias had told the guards outside his room that he needed a midnight snack. He didn't know what excuse Nina had used, but he wished it were one that involved a warmer location.

"Can I go with you when you explain the idea to everyone else?" Matthias asked as he tried to hold back his shivers.

Nina frowned. In the ghostly light of the freezer, this cast ghoulish shadows across her face.

"It's not like I'm going to call a meeting," Nina said. "I'll pass a note to—well, my contact. My contact will pass a note to his contact. And so on."

"But who'll make the final decision?" Matthias asked.

"It's safer if I don't tell you," Nina said. "Safer for you, safer for us."

The shadows of Nina's eye sockets frightened Matthias. The chill of the freezer reminded him of running through snowy fields in search of help for Percy and Alia. An act of desperate hope that he now knew had been all for nothing.

"Nina," he began, but the words he wanted to say were frozen inside him. He couldn't tell her how badly he wanted this plan to succeed, because everything else he'd tried to do had failed.

"I'll get back to you as soon as I can," she said, her hand already on the door latch. "It might be a day or two."

"A day or two?" Matthias repeated incredulously. "The ceremony's next Friday."

"All this passing notes takes a while," Nina said, and she slipped out the door.

Matthias went back to bed, but he couldn't sleep. He stared into the darkness, missing Percy, missing Alia, missing Samuel.

Can I trust Nina? he wanted to ask them. *Am I doing the right thing?*

The next few days seemed unbearably long. Matthias haunted the cafeteria, but Nina looked straight through him as she handed him nothing but bowls and plates. He forced himself to listen to the headphones as much as possible, but all the commander's planning seemed to be finished; Matthias heard little but the scratching of pen on paper, the soft rustle of papers being shifted from side to side.

What if all the interesting conversations are taking place when I'm not listening? Matthias tortured himself wondering. *What if they've finished Project Exchange early and the ceremony's this week and we don't even know?*

The commander visited Matthias every night, right before bedtime, and it was all Matthias could do not to blurt out, *I hear there's some big ceremony coming up soon. When is it? What's it for?* But it was safer to act dumb, to pretend there was nothing on his mind except grief.

"How are your studies coming along?" the commander asked one evening as he sat on the edge of Matthias's bed.

"Huh?" Matthias said.

The commander pointed to the headphones and tape recorder on the bedside table.

"Your classes? Remember?"

"Oh." Matthias thought fast. "I try to listen, but I start thinking about Tiddy and then I miss half the tape so I have to start it all over again."

The commander touched Matthias's cheek.

"I understand," he said sorrowfully.

Matthias lowered his eyes and mumbled, "I'll try harder."

The next morning he did slip a cassette into the recorder, but it started out, "All our country's problems can be traced to the evil of the third children, those who harbor this scourge, and those who provide fake identification to encourage their prodigal ways. . . ."

Matthias couldn't bear to listen to any more. He clicked off the recorder and went down to breakfast.

And this time when Nina handed him a bowl of Cream of Wheat, he felt a thin edge of paper under the rim. It was so hard not to drop the bowl and read the note, right there in front of the entire cafeteria. He managed to walk to his table with studied carelessness, but once there he couldn't help unfolding the paper in his lap, glancing down quickly: *When you get back to your room, you'll find your weapon on your bed.*

"Hey, little buddy, mind if I sit with you?"

It was Tiddy's friend Mike. Quickly, Matthias crammed Nina's note into his pocket.

"S-Sure," Matthias stammered, but inside he was thinking, *Did Mike see the note? He couldn't have, he's on the other side of the table. But what if he did? What if he knows all about me and the plan?* Then, *Weapon? WEAPON? Would Samuel approve of me using a weapon?*

"Haven't seen you around much," Mike was saying. "I've been out on patrol a lot. Man, it's cold out there. It'll be nice when spring gets here. . . ."

"Uh-huh," Matthias said, and "You're right," but he wasn't really listening as Mike rambled on.

Then Mike said, "I see you've got your eye on one of the serving girls. Cute one, huh?"

"What?" Matthias asked, suddenly panicked. He realized he had been looking toward Nina, but he hadn't meant to. "I'm not—I mean—"

Mike laughed.

"Hey, didn't mean to embarrass you. You're blushing.

It's okay, she's not bad-looking. But I'll warn you: I've seen her passing love notes to other guys. Slips it into their hands with their soup bowls. Very clever. She passing love notes to you yet?"

Matthias froze. How much did Mike know? How could Matthias possibly answer that question?

Oh, please, God, help me, Matthias prayed silently as beads of sweat broke out on his forehead.

Suddenly Matthias knew what to say.

"Is she passing love notes to you?" he challenged Mike. "Did you come over here to warn me away from your girlfriend?"

"I wish," Mike said, laughing again. And then he changed the subject.

Matthias finished breakfast as quickly as he could. He wanted to warn Nina that Mike had seen her passing notes, but he didn't know how he could do it without attracting more attention. And he was worried about having a weapon lying out on his bed. He raced up the stairs and burst into his room. A large orange sphere sat in the middle of his comforter.

His "weapon" was a basketball.

CHAPTER *THIRTY-FOUR*

No!" Matthias wailed at Nina.

This time they were hiding in a closet just inside the cafeteria in the middle of the night. With his elbow jammed into a stack of dishtowels and his feet planted in a scrub bucket, Matthias knew he was going to have a hard time getting Nina to take him seriously. He tried anyway.

"This was my idea! I don't want to be just a . . . a decoy!"

"Shh," Nina said. "Someone's going to hear you." She shook her head and pulled the door completely shut. Now they were in total darkness. Nina bent over and whispered directly into Matthias's ear. "You can't just think about what *you* want. Everybody notices you, because of Tiddy. If you disappeared, it'd make a big stir. Besides, if your plan works, we need you to keep eavesdropping on the commander's office."

Matthias imagined his future as Nina saw it: He'd lie on his bed for the rest of his life listening to the bug from the commander's office. No—eventually the commander would expect Matthias to start attending the meetings. Eventually Matthias would have to start acting like a true member of the Population Police. Start hurting people, killing people—joining in their evil.

He'd have to do that, or the rest of his life would not be very long.

"Nina, I can't go on eavesdropping," Matthias whispered back, his words sinking into the darkness. He wished he and Nina were in full sunshine; he thought that maybe if she could see his face, she'd understand that he wasn't just being selfish by wanting to get away from Population Police headquarters. "Give the tape recorder and headphones to someone else—anyone in the building should be able to pick up the signals."

"Without getting caught?" Nina challenged.

Matthias shrugged helplessly, forgetting Nina couldn't see him. He'd gotten distracted from what he really wanted to say.

"Nina, you knew Percy and Alia," he began. "You know what great friends they were. You know they never had the chance to eat all the food they ever wanted, to wear nice clothes, to be treated like . . . like some sort of precious toy. Like I'm being treated now. But they didn't ever have to act like an evil man is their best friend, either, or pretend to be grieving for a killer. Remember how nice Alia always was to you when Percy and I still weren't sure we could trust you? She wasn't pretending. She really liked you, and she always wanted to believe that people are good, underneath it all."

Matthias stopped because the words were getting caught in his throat. There was a silence, and he was afraid that Nina hadn't even heard him.

Then, "What's that got to do with your role in the plan?" Nina asked. She sounded like she was trying to stay harsh and businesslike, but she had a catch in her voice.

"Nothing. Everything," Matthias said. "It may not make sense to you, but I have to do this. For Percy and Alia." *And Samuel*, he thought. *And Mrs. Talbot. And the seventeen rebels I saw the Population Police kill.* His memory stretched back even further. Maybe he needed to do this for two other people as well—a man and a woman who'd been so terrified of the Population Police's power that they'd left their baby on a doorstep in a dark alley.

"I think—," Nina began, and Matthias could tell her answer was going to be no. She had to have everything making sense; she wouldn't let his emotions overrule her carefully plotted reasons.

And then suddenly the closet door whipped open, and two Population Police guards were shining flashlights right at them.

CHAPTER THIRTY-FIVE

"Too bad. We didn't catch them kissing," one of the guards said.

It was Mike. He stood there leering at the two of them, the lights of the cafeteria blazing behind him.

"The kid keeps saying he needs a midnight snack. The girl always says she has extra work to do," the other guard said, shaking his head. "And I'm supposed to believe them?"

Too late, Matthias realized that this was the same guard who had been on duty the last time he'd sneaked down to meet Nina. The guard reached out and grabbed the back of Matthias's shirt collar. Mike took hold of Nina's collar too and pulled her out of the closet.

"Think the commander will be interested in hearing about this?" the guard asked. "Think he'd give me a reward?"

"Or a swift kick," Mike mused. He steered Nina by the collar until she was right beside Matthias. "Don't you think they're cute together? It'd be kind of a shame to thwart young love. And you've got to give the kid credit for winning over an older lady."

Nina and Matthias stood stiffly, side by side, frozen in fear.

"But the commander—," the guard said.

"The commander just lost Tiddy," Mike said. "You want to be the reason he stops trusting the kid?"

Nina tore away from Mike's grasp and fell to her knees.

"Please," she begged. "Punish me if you have to. But don't—don't tell on my boyfriend." She lowered her head, and Matthias could see tears glistening in her eyelashes.

"See?" Mike said. "How can you resist that?"

"But what if they're—," the other guard began.

"What?" Mike asked. "Spies? Saboteurs? Rebels? Con men? Give me a break. They're just a couple of kids. In love. Don't you remember the first girl you kissed?"

The guard got a dreamy look on his face, then he shrugged it away.

"Okay, okay," he muttered. "I won't say anything this time. But if I ever catch the two of you sneaking down here in the middle of the night again, you're in big trouble. Now go on back to your rooms."

He shoved Matthias forward and Matthias fell over, sprawled out on the floor. As Matthias was scrambling back to his feet, he heard Mike say, "Oh, at least let them hug each other good-bye."

Mike stood back looking thoroughly entertained as

Matthias awkwardly put his arms around Nina's shoulders. She was still on her knees, so Matthias had to bend over. He kept his head on the side away from Mike and the other guard, so he dared to bury his face in Nina's hair and whisper into her ear, "You have to let me go with you now. Now that they suspect—"

"Okay! That's enough!" the guard called out.

Nina pulled away and stood up. Matthias could see the tears welling in her eyes, the red marks on her neck where Mike had pulled her collar too hard, the individual hairs that had escaped from her braids and reached out toward Matthias like they had a mind of their own. And he could see her head moving slowly, up and down.

She was saying yes.

CHAPTER *THIRTY-SIX*

At dusk the next day, Matthias took his basketball and stepped out of his room, latching the door firmly behind him. Nina's new instructions—which she'd passed to him at lunch—had reminded him to act carefree and playful; he just hoped he could keep his legs from shaking. Ever since he and Nina had been caught in the closet, he'd been imagining all the ways this plan could go wrong.

God? he prayed. *Are you with me?*

He strolled past all the guards in the hallway. One of them winked at him, and he didn't understand why. Was the guard trying to warn Matthias somehow? Did the guard know something that Matthias didn't? Or was the wink just because the guard had heard about Matthias being caught in a closet with a girl? People acted like that sometimes about boys and girls falling in love. Matthias didn't understand it. He didn't want to. Love made him think of the way Mr. Talbot had acted, saying good-bye to his wife when she'd gone to help Percy and Alia. Right at the end, Mr. Talbot had let his fingers linger on the side of the car, as if he couldn't bear to let her go. And then she hadn't come back. . . .

Because I led her into danger. My fault, Matthias thought.

He couldn't think about that right now. Too distracting. He forced himself to walk down the stairs, out the front door, and several feet down the driveway. So far, so good. He positioned himself near the line of guards at the front gate and began bouncing the ball.

"Anyone want to play with me?" he asked.

Surely it didn't matter that his voice came out sounding so plaintive. Surely the guards would interpret that as his longing for Tiddy, not his fear of being caught in a subversive plot.

Several of the guards looked down at him and smiled indulgently. Matthias saw a few of them elbow one another.

"We're busy. Sorry," one of them said, not unkindly.

Matthias kept bouncing his ball. He'd actually never played with a basketball before; he'd never before touched one that wasn't crushed and tossed out in the trash. Matthias was surprised at how quickly this ball bounced back up, how hard it smacked his hand.

Just bouncing the ball's not good enough, he reminded himself.

"Watch this," he said, and tried to balance the ball on the tip of his finger. He was supposed to make the ball spin, but he couldn't even get it to wobble. It kept falling off and rolling down against the guards' feet. They kept gently kicking the ball back to Matthias. Then one of the guards picked it up.

"I'll show you how it's done," he said. He placed the ball on his finger and sent it whirling.

"Wow," Matthias breathed out, and his awe wasn't faked. How could anyone do that?

"Oh, that's nothing. You should see Chester from over in the control room," the guard said. "Hey, Jim, go tell Chester to come out here for a minute."

Another guard walked over to a booth right at the gateway. An unbelievably tall guard poked his head out of the booth's doorway.

"Yeah?" he said.

"The kid wants to see a basketball demonstration."

The tall guard—Chester—glanced down at some monitor in the control booth, then stepped out.

"I guess I could do a quick show," he said.

He leaned down and scooped up the ball. It seemed to jump from one hand to the other, now spinning, now running down Chester's arms and across his shoulders, now bouncing from back to front between his legs. Matthias watched, amazed, and cheered along with the other Population Police guards.

But Matthias kept only one eye on Chester's stunning show. He was also watching the control booth.

Nobody had stepped in to take Chester's place.

A few minutes later, Chester caught the ball behind his

back on the toe of his shoe and took a huge bow. Then he tossed the ball toward Matthias.

"Okay, back to work," he said reluctantly.

Matthias fumbled trying to catch the ball. It rolled back toward Chester.

Just a few more seconds, Matthias thought. *Show off just a little bit more.*

But Chester kept walking toward the control booth.

Matthias leaned down to pick up the ball himself. He was glad he was facing the ground so he didn't have to keep the glee out of his expression when Chester cried out, "What? Our monitors are down! So's the electric fence!"

Other guards rushed in behind Chester. They were punching buttons, shouting into walkie-talkies. Matthias thought it was safe to wander over behind them and stand on tiptoe to get a glimpse of the defective monitors.

A walkie-talkie crackled.

"Found the problem. Some animal chewed through two wires back here. We'll have them fixed in a few minutes."

Matthias put his hands over his mouth and tried to look horrified, but he was hiding a grin. Alia had been the one who'd taught Nina that make-it-look-like-an-animal-chewed-the-wire trick.

It wasn't long before Chester's monitor screens flickered back to life. From his vantage point, Matthias could tell that the screens showed long stretches of the stone wall and electric fence that completely surrounded

Population Police headquarters. He caught no glimpse of shadowy figures climbing through.

That means the others are out! he thought joyfully. *Or . . . maybe they couldn't make it in time and gave up.*

He had no way of knowing which was true. All he could do was stick with his part of the plan.

The guards resumed their strict, straight-line formation. Matthias went back to bouncing his basketball. He made a few feeble attempts at some of Chester's tricks. The basketball refused to roll in a smooth line down Matthias's arms; it banged his shin rather than jumping smoothly under his leg.

"That toe trick looked cool," Matthias said.

He turned around, took a deep breath, and tossed the ball over his shoulder. He glanced back and saw the ball sail out into the open air, past the line of guards, past the control booth, past the gate. It hit the ground and started rolling, beyond the boundaries of Population Police headquarters.

"Oops," Matthias said. "I'll get that."

This was the decisive moment. If one of the guards said, *No, you're not allowed, I'll get it,* or *No, too bad, your ball's gone for good,* or *I forbid you to go out there,* then all would be lost and Matthias might be stuck at Population Police headquarters forever. The thought seemed more unbearable than ever. The very air around Matthias seemed to cage him—air that any minute might carry words to his ears that he desperately did not want to hear. . . .

Nobody said anything.

Matthias trotted after his ball, past the guards, past the control booth, past the gate.

Nobody objected. He'd been set free by a child's toy.

When Matthias reached the place where the ball had come to rest against a tuft of frozen grass, he faked clumsiness, kicking the ball and sending it even farther beyond the gate. It rolled into thick woods that had sunk into near darkness now. Matthias could barely see, but that was good—the guards wouldn't be able to see him now either.

He peered around for a pinprick of light in the darkness—*Oh, please, let the others be waiting*—and there it was, a tiny red glow off to the right.

Matthias crashed through the woods, not worrying about the noise, just concentrating on speed. How long did he have before one of the guards came out looking for him?

He was closer to the red light now. It was coming from inside a long, dark car parked on a dirt road in the shadows. Matthias covered the last few yards in a mad rush. He yanked on the door handle of the car and dived through the opening.

"Go!" he burst out before he'd shut the door, before he'd seen who was holding the light, whom he'd landed next to.

"Sure thing," a voice drawled, and the car shot forward into the dark night.

Matthias jerked the door shut, and it dawned on him:

He knew that voice. He looked over, squinting into the darkness. The driver was illuminated only in the glow from the dashboard, but Matthias recognized his face.

It was Mike.

CHAPTER THIRTY-SEVEN

You?" Matthias asked. He glanced around frantically. The rest of the car was empty. "Where's—?" He stopped himself just in time. He couldn't give away Nina and Trey.

"Relax," Mike said. "I'm on your side. Didn't you figure that out when I gave you and Nina that great cover story last night?"

Now that Matthias thought about it, Mike had tried awfully hard to keep the other guard from telling the commander.

"I thought you were just obsessed with people having girlfriends," Matthias muttered.

Mike chuckled.

"Everyone wants to believe in love," he said. "Even ugly Population Police guards."

Mike was speeding up. He rounded a bend and hit a straightaway that allowed him to zoom through the woods. Matthias looked cautiously over his shoulder. No

182 · M A R G A R E T P E T E R S O N H A D D I X

headlights were following them—maybe Matthias could dare to believe that he'd get away safely.

That is, if he was safe with Mike.

"Are we meeting Nina and the others somewhere else?" Matthias asked hesitantly. Mike obviously knew about Nina; it wouldn't be a betrayal to mention just her name.

"Nope," Mike said.

"But the plan—"

"We had to modify it a little," Mike said. "It took everyone working together just to get you and me away from headquarters. Someone to watch you at the front gate and signal the person cutting the wires, someone to plant the dead squirrel beside the cut wires, someone to hide this car outside the fence . . . We're just hoping that everyone back at HQ is so busy looking for you that they don't check out any of the other suspicious activities this afternoon."

"Oh," Matthias said.

He still wished Nina were with them, or someone else he was sure he could trust. He shrank lower in his seat. The car was going so fast now, it made him feel a little sick.

"You think the two of us can do everything in time?" Matthias asked.

"Of course not," Mike said calmly. "We're getting help with that. From people who *aren't* on our side."

"What?" Matthias asked, thoroughly confused now.

"There's a zipper on the left side of your seat," Mike said. "It's hard to find, but if you can, open it and pull out one of the flyers."

Matthias obediently felt along the side of his leather seat. The zipper was in a seam near the top, and its teeth gave way reluctantly as Matthias pulled on it. By feel, he found, first, foam stuffing and then a stack of hundreds of papers. He eased one out.

"Here," Mike said, handing Matthias the penlight.

Matthias switched it on and directed the tiny red glow at the paper. In huge letters at the top, the paper read:

THE POPULATION POLICE NEED YOUR HELP!
Smaller type below proclaimed:

Under the leadership of President Aldous Krakenaur, we have uncovered a plot to steal and/or destroy food that rightfully belongs to all the legal citizens of this great nation. With your assistance, we can protect our food supply. We need all loyal citizens from your sector to go to 108 Warehouse Row at 1:00 a.m. on February 2. . . .

The red light and the tiny words made Matthias feel queasier than ever. He shook his head dizzily.

"This can't be right," he said.

"Why not?" Mike asked.

"This makes it sound like the Population Police are the good guys," Matthias said. "Like they're just trying to protect the food from the rebels. Us. That's wrong—we're the ones who want to hand the food out."

Mike took his eyes off the road long enough to shoot a sharp glance at Matthias.

"And what do you think the people would do if we

passed out notes saying, 'The rebels invite you to take food away from the Population Police'?" Mike asked. "Do you think anybody would show up? I don't know about you, but I think *I'd* cower in my bed. *I'd* avoid Warehouse Row as if my life depended on it."

Mike had a mocking tone in his voice—it was almost like he was mocking Matthias's original idea.

"And there aren't enough of us rebels to pass out all the notes in time," Mike continued. "No, we have to do this under the guise of the Population Police. It's the only way this can work."

Matthias was still shaking his head.

"But . . . does the commander know? Does the president?" he asked.

"Of course not," Mike said. "We're using flunkies who are supposed to think that I'm a top-ranking officer."

Matthias noticed that Mike had extra medals and ribbons pinned to his chest, extra patches sewn to his arm.

More lies, Matthias thought. He'd seen the food giveaway as something straightforward: *Here, poor people, take this food that the Population Police have been keeping from you. Go and starve no more.* But his plan had been tweaked and twisted almost beyond recognition. Did he even want to be a part of the plan now?

What else could he do?

Matthias didn't say anything.

They were out of the woods now and on the outskirts of the city. Burned-out, tumbledown houses gave way to tidy streets. Mike pulled up alongside a low, newly white-washed building with a glittering sign out front proclaiming, POPULATION POLICE SUBSTATION—EASTERN BRANCH.

"Just when I get away from one Population Police head-quarters, we go straight to another one?" Matthias moaned.

"Stick close by me and keep your mouth shut," Mike said. "They're supposed to think you're my servant. So you get to carry all the flyers."

It took Matthias four trips to transport all the papers from the car to a long row of tables inside a meeting room. The job took even longer because each time he went into or out of the building, he had to sign in or sign out and pass through a security screening. Each time Matthias scrawled, *Roger Symmes* on the security pad, he was certain someone would scream out, *Wait! You're the kid who's missing from main headquarters!*

But all the guards were watching Mike. Matthias got the feeling that this particular substation had never received a visit from such a decorated officer before.

"I need all your men assembled in the briefing room!" Mike roared. "Now!"

"Um, some of them are sleeping, like if they're going to be on guard duty overnight—," a guard timidly started to explain.

Mike cut him off. "I said everyone! Now!"

By the time Matthias had all the flyers lined up on the

tables, the room was overflowing with men in uniform—some of them, indeed, looking as though they'd just been awakened. Mike strode to the front of the room, and the room instantly became silent.

"This is an emergency!" Mike screamed.

He gave a quick explanation of the supposed crisis, making the "rebels" who intended to destroy the food supply sound so vile and disgusting that Matthias began picturing them with horns and forked tails.

"My assistant will pass out street assignments for each of you," Mike said, handing Matthias yet another stack of papers. "Go to every habitation—every house, every apartment, every makeshift shed—and give the people their orders for picking up the food."

"But what if the people eat the food?" someone asked.

"Oh, they won't dare do that. They'll know that we're keeping track, and we'll know if they don't return it after the crisis has passed," Mike said. "Is that clear?"

Standing behind Mike, Matthias could see drops of sweat trickling down the back of his neck. But his voice came out clear and confident.

"Why don't we just catch the rebels?" an officer in the front row dared to ask. "Wouldn't that be easier?"

"It's too late for that," Mike burst out. "And—and we can't take any chances with our food supply."

"Then I'll call for reinforcements," the officer said. He reached for a telephone Matthias hadn't noticed before. Matthias watched with a sinking feeling as the officer put the receiver to his ear, reached down to dial . . . and stopped. "That's odd," he said. "Phone's dead."

Mike's face seemed to turn stark white.

"The rebels cut the wires!" he screamed. "They found out which station we're using! Hurry! Get your assignments and go!"

Pandemonium broke out. The men swarmed forward, grabbing their assignments from Matthias and stacks of flyers from the table. Matthias was sure he'd be crushed. But moments later, he and Mike were left alone in the midst of overturned chairs, flipped tables, ripped papers. Through the window, he could see cars and trucks careening out into the street, their tires squealing.

"Okay, now we head to the warehouse," Mike said calmly.

Back in the car, Matthias dared to ask, "You cut the phone lines yourself, didn't you? How'd you do that when they were watching you the whole time?"

"Maybe we had a friend or two at that substation, after all," Mike said.

Matthias frowned and watched the dark street glide by outside his window for a few minutes.

"Why can't you just tell me?" he finally said, turning back to Mike. "Nina always keeps secrets from me, and it drives me crazy. 'No, I can't tell you that. It isn't safe.' 'It's better if you don't know any other names. . . .'"

"Nina's right," Mike said. "Secrecy is safer. If our plan works, if you and I both survive the night . . . Well, we wouldn't want to get anyone else in trouble."

Mike thinks we're going to be caught, Matthias realized. *Caught and tortured, probably, until we tell on all of our friends. And then, once again, I'll have hurt someone trying to do something good. Or maybe not . . .* Something new occurred to him.

"I don't know your last name," Matthias said, startled at the thought. "I don't know what name Nina was using at Population Police headquarters. I don't know the name on anyone's I.D. card."

"Good," Mike said grimly, staring straight ahead. "Let's keep it that way."

They arrived at the warehouse. The same collection of trash-covered lumps were scattered along the wall, but this time Matthias recognized them as human right away.

"Let's hope they haven't changed the password," Mike muttered. "Why don't you give it, since you've been here before."

With Mike at his side, Matthias stepped up to the intercom. His hand trembled as he pressed the button.

"Glorious future," he squeaked.

The door opened slowly, as if the guard wasn't quite sure about Matthias. Mike barreled his way through the cracked door, his fists flailing. In seconds, he'd knocked the guard out flat on the floor. Mike stabbed a hypodermic needle into the guard's arm.

"That'll make sure he stays unconscious," Mike said. "Now, let's just hope there really was only one guard. . . ."

Mike slipped a key ring from the guard's belt, and the two of them raced through the building, checking behind every door. There were four levels to the building, so it took a long time. But the building had a simple layout: Every door on the left side of the building led to the food storeroom; every door on the right side led to a room containing hundreds and thousands of white cards—the I.D.'s.

But Mike and Matthias found no other people anywhere else in the building.

"Good thing the commander was so paranoid about secrecy," Mike muttered as they returned to the first floor. "Only one guard for this entire building—it's crazy."

They moved the unconscious guard's body into an alcove off the entryway.

"This way, he won't get trampled," Mike said. "Things are going to be pretty chaotic." He glanced at his watch. "It's a shame I didn't set the times a little earlier. The first group of people won't start arriving to carry away the food for another hour."

"No," Matthias said. "I bet we can have some in here in five minutes."

"How?" Mike asked.

But Matthias was already bounding out the doors, ready to wake up the people sleeping on the street.

CHAPTER *THIRTY-EIGHT*

The next several hours passed in a complete blur. The starving people from the streets came in first, stumbling and rubbing their eyes and squinting as if they couldn't believe the sight before them.

"Take as much food as you can carry," Matthias told them, again and again. "Then run as far away from here as you can!"

They were all gone before the first group of people showed up holding the fake Population Police flyers. These people were used to standing in line; they were used to being handed measly portions of grain or small lumps of mealy bread. They couldn't seem to understand, "Take as much as you can." They couldn't seem to understand, "Grab anything! Go!"

With each group that came in, Matthias watched the emotions play over people's faces: first astonishment and disbelief, then craftiness, then unbridled glee. A carnival atmosphere took over the storeroom. Word seemed to spread between the groups that were leaving and the ones arriving; some people in the later groups brought young children, and Matthias overheard parents telling little boys and girls, "This is how grocery stores looked when I was a kid. And we could go there anytime we wanted. . . ."

Matthias was just glad to see the food disappearing from the shelves.

By 6:00 A.M., all the food had vanished from the lower levels. The metal walkways leading to the upper levels got so crowded that people had to reach out from ladders; they had to balance on wobbly rungs while they shoved peaches and apples and potatoes into their pockets. This slowed everyone down, but Matthias didn't think it mattered until Mike came and whispered into his ear, "We need to clear this place out in five minutes."

"Why?" Matthias asked.

"News got back to headquarters," Mike said. "The commander's on his way over right now."

"Everybody out!" Matthias shouted.

"The building's going to explode!" Mike hollered behind him.

That got people running. Some jumped off ladders from five rungs up. Some of the Population Police officers who had handed out the flyers were standing around the doors, and they were the first ones out, clutching loaves of bread and cartons of milk.

"Why'd you say that?" Matthias asked Mike as they were carried along in the stampede for the doors.

"Because it's true!" Mike said. "Run! Get as far away from here as you can!"

Mike grabbed Matthias's arm and jerked him along with the crowd, but a man carrying a huge bag of potatoes smashed in between them. Matthias landed on the floor, out of the way of all the feet trampling toward the exits. He blinked up dizzily at the lights; the nearly empty shelves overhead seemed to sway in and out of his line of sight.

The building's going to explode? Is that really true or just another of Mike's lies? Why would it explode?

Then Matthias remembered the roomful of I.D.'s. He remembered Project Exchange and Project Authenticity and the fact that the storeroom of food was the only thing that had kept the rebels from trying to destroy the I.D.'s before. But the food was mostly gone now, except for a stray rotten apple or two here and there.

Matthias struggled to his feet. He fought his way back into the crowd, squeezed through a doorway and along the hall. And then suddenly fresh air hit his face and, oddly, there was sunlight.

People were screaming and running and some of them had dropped their food. Matthias grabbed a heap of potatoes and stuffed them in his pocket. He saw Mike standing across the street—the only person just standing, not running. Mike caught Matthias's eye and smiled and nodded, and then Mike turned his head and seemed to be whispering something into his collar. He waved his hand toward Matthias, beckoning him away from the warehouse.

Matthias remembered how the man in the tree back by the cabin had tried to wave him away from danger. Matthias hadn't understood, but the entire world had seemed to explode into gunfire only seconds later. Matthias glanced behind him and saw that the stream of people running out of the warehouse had stopped. Everyone was out now. Everyone was safe. Except—

Matthias remembered the guard. The guard Mike had knocked unconscious and hidden in an alcove.

Matthias turned and darted back into the building. He thought he could hear Mike across the street yelling, "No! Come back!" but he kept going. His footsteps echoed in the now-deserted hallway. He found the guard and grabbed him under the armpits and tugged and tugged. But the guard was much larger and heavier than Matthias, so his progress was slow. Matthias strained harder, his pulse throbbing in his ears as if counting off the seconds he had left.

Matthias reached the doorway to the outdoors, and the sunlight blinded him temporarily. The street seemed to be empty now, except for one car pulled up to the bottom of the stairs and one man stepping out of it.

One man. The commander.

"You?" the commander said, his voice a mix of bafflement and pain.

Matthias shoved the guard's body forward. It rolled

down the stairs, gaining momentum until it slammed into the commander, knocking him back against the car. Matthias didn't have time to watch what happened next. He could hear rumblings behind him. He hurdled the railing and dived underneath the car, sliding into position between the two front tires.

And then the warehouse collapsed, raining bricks down everywhere.

CHAPTER *THIRTY-NINE*

You idiot! Were you trying to get yourself killed?"
Mike's voice.

Matthias moaned and opened his eyes. He didn't feel entirely certain that he *hadn't* been killed, until his eyes focused in the dim light. He was encased in blankets but seemed to be lying on the floor in a huge room. The ceiling arced high overhead.

"What—don't you like the fancy hospital I brought you to?" Mike asked. "We're in another warehouse, but don't worry—this one's abandoned and in no danger of falling down." He glanced around a little nervously. "As far as I know."

Matthias squinted, trying to figure out how he and Mike had gotten to this dark, silent place after all the noise and confusion and people running and screaming and bricks falling. . . .

"You . . . exploded the other warehouse," Matthias mumbled, remembering. "And all the I.D.'s . . ."

"Well, imploded, technically," Mike said. "We tried to rig it so the building would fall inward, instead of bursting outward. We were trying to minimize the risk to innocent bystanders. But, yeah, all the I.D.'s were destroyed. The only identity anyone in this country has now is a paper receipt. And *everyone* has that. Legal citizens. Illegal third children. Wanted criminals. It's going to take the Population Police a long time to sort everyone out. If they ever can."

Mike sounded so gleeful that Matthias winced.

"But you wanted the guard to die?" Matthias asked. "And the commander?"

"Honestly, I forgot about the guard," Mike said, a troubled look in his eye. "But the commander . . . We weren't trying to kill him, but I wouldn't have complained if he'd been standing right in that doorway when the building fell."

Where he probably would have been if I hadn't distracted him, if I hadn't thrown the guard's body at him, Matthias thought.

"Did . . . did they both die?" Matthias asked.

"Don't know," Mike said. "I pulled you out of the rubble and ran. I have some . . . friends who ought to bring me some updates soon."

But Matthias's eyes were closing again. He slid back into a strangely untroubled sleep. *I got away from Population Police headquarters. We gave the food away. I did my best to save the guard's life. It's time to rest.*

Over the next few days, Matthias slid in and out of

consciousness. He woke once feeling warm and cozy, and he discovered that Mike had found or built a small stove that radiated heat into their tiny section of the huge warehouse. The next time he woke, Mike spooned hot, cooked potato into his mouth.

"Smart of you to think to pick up some of the food yourself," Mike said as he fed Matthias. "I left with nothing. Didn't want to think about afterward, I guess. Couldn't believe there would be an afterward."

"Nobody caught us," Matthias said. "We're still alive."

"For now," Mike said, glancing nervously over his shoulder, into darkness. "Still haven't heard from my friends."

When Matthias woke again, sunlight was fighting its way through the dirty glass panes overhead, and Mike was missing. Matthias sat up dizzily, straining sore muscles. He hadn't even thought to ask exactly how he'd been injured. Gingerly, he felt his arms and legs. He discovered plenty of bruises, but none of the bones were broken. His chest ached, though, and when he looked, he saw that he had several extra layers of cloth wrapped around his torso.

"Why? Cracked rib?" Matthias wondered aloud.

And then Mike was there, grinning in the sunlight.

"Don't worry—you're healing fast. And guess what? You're a hero now!"

"Huh?" Matthias said.

Mike sat down on a rusted pipe beside Matthias's makeshift bed.

"I finally got to talk to my contact," Mike said. "You won't believe how everything turned out. We're heroes to the Population Police. They're writing commemorative poems about us. There's even talk of erecting a statue!"

"What?"

"I know—it sounds too incredible," Mike said, so exuberant that he practically bounced in his seat. "But everyone still believes that bogus story I made up about uncovering the plot to blow up the warehouse and not having time to alert headquarters and just doing everything I could to save the food. Nobody quite understands how you ended up helping me, but they don't care about the details since you saved the commander's life."

"I did?" Matthias asked dazedly.

"Yeah, he and the guard both survived."

Mike's tone was grudging, and Matthias felt confused.

I didn't want anyone to die. But what if the commander's death had meant that a lot of other people got to live? Matthias wondered. He didn't know what to think about the commander, anyway. *How could he have been so nice to me and so cruel in his job?*

Mike was still talking.

"At least, you're getting *some* of the credit for saving the commander's life. There are all these wild rumors going around about how people supposedly saw the ghost of Tiddy with you there at the end, when you were getting the guard out—because how else could a little boy like you carry a two-hundred-pound man?"

Matthias gaped at Mike.

"A ghost? That's crazy," he said indignantly. "Anyhow, I didn't carry the guard—I dragged him."

"I know," Mike agreed. "But those rumors just make us look better."

Matthias frowned.

"Aren't the Population Police mad at us for giving away all that food?"

"Oh, no," Mike said. "They're proud of us for saving it. Because—get this—people brought it back!"

Mike laughed delightedly, and Matthias was sure he'd heard wrong.

"They brought it back? Why?"

"Because that's what it said on the flyers, that they were just supposed to take care of the food temporarily, until the Population Police could eradicate the threat," Mike said. "So people started returning everything to another warehouse the very next day."

Matthias stared at Mike in dismay.

"But . . . I wanted the people to keep the food. They were starving!"

"Well, that first group you brought in, I bet they ate the food right away," Mike said. "And the Population Police will never be able to track *them* down. So that turned out all right."

"But the other people, the ones who brought the food back—how could they be so stupid? How could they ruin our plan like that?" In his indignation, Matthias forgot his sore muscles and his cracked rib and gestured wildly. His arm swung out and knocked against a pile of junk metal, which toppled to the ground with a horrible racket.

Matthias froze, and Mike glanced around fearfully.

"We're still in hiding—remember?" he said.

"But—but—," Matthias sputtered.

Mike glanced around again and seemed to decide no one was going to show up to investigate the noise.

"Try to understand," he said. "People have been living with the Population Police for a long time. It's like they've been trained to believe that the only way for them to survive is to do what the Government says. What good is a bag of potatoes if it means that you'll be hunted down, taken out at dawn, and shot? You see what we're up against, trying to win a little freedom. The people we're trying to win it for don't remember what freedom is."

Matthias shook his head, still angry.

"Then it was all for nothing, what we did," he said.

"You can't believe that," Mike said, and an edge of anger had crept into his voice as well. "We destroyed the I.D.'s, remember? *Without* destroying the food!"

Matthias looked down at the packed-dirt floor. He didn't think he could explain. Destroying the I.D.'s was complicated—what if the Population Police managed to dig them out of the ruins and continued with Project Authenticity anyhow? What if the Population Police had duplicate records elsewhere that made it possible for them to find and kill all the third children regardless of everything Mike and Matthias and the others had done to stop them?

But giving away the food had seemed simple. That had been his tribute to the memory of Percy, Alia, and Samuel. In their memory, starving people would be fed.

Only it wasn't much of a tribute if the hungry people had just given the food right back to the Population Police.

"I don't know what your life was like before Tiddy brought you to Population Police headquarters," Mike said softly. "But after Tiddy died, after the commander decided you were his surrogate son in Tiddy's place, you had it made. You could have asked the commander for anything, and he would have given it to you. Most people in a situation like that would have eaten it up—all the gourmet food, all the luxuries the commander would provide. They would have done everything in their power to keep that cozy life.

"But you didn't," Mike went on, his voice practically a whisper now. "You walked away from all of that to do what you thought was right. You even risked your life to save a man everyone else had forgotten about." He bent his face in close to Matthias's, and his voice became even more intense. "You cannot say that was for nothing."

Matthias shook his head, not to disagree, but because he was confused.

"Every time I try to do something good, it gets messed up," he complained.

"That's life," Mike said, shrugging. "You in for another round?"

"What?" Matthias asked.

"I'm going to wait a few days, make sure everything shakes out," Mike said. "Then I'm going back to Population Police headquarters. Our job isn't done until every last person in this country is free. You coming with me?"

Matthias jerked back so violently, he almost knocked over another pile of junk. Go back to Population Police headquarters? He'd never dreamed that anybody would ask him to do such a thing. He'd never dreamed that it'd be possible to step foot anywhere near a Population Police officer without being arrested and executed on the spot. His stomach churned at the thought of being in the midst of all that evil and intrigue again, of having to smile adoringly at the commander while secretly hating everything the commander stood for.

But that wasn't the reason he shook his head at Mike.

"No," Matthias said. "There's something else I have to do."

CHAPTER *FORTY*

The truck chugged through the night, its headlights casting eerie shadows. Matthias had no idea where Mike had gotten the truck—or the slips of paper that passed for identification at every checkpoint.

"This is all we have," Mike said apologetically each time the Population Police stopped them.

"It's all anyone has anymore," the Population Police officers muttered back. "Just wait till we find those rebels. . . ."

"I know what you mean," Mike always said sympathetically. But as soon as the officers waved him on through the checkpoint, he'd start giggling. "Did you hear that? We were right under their nose, and they didn't even know it! Man, I love these paper I.D.'s!"

Matthias couldn't join in Mike's mirth. He sat quietly, peering into the darkness, waiting for a small cottage to come into view.

He and Mike were wearing civilian clothes again. Mike's

were ordinary jeans and a sweatshirt that one of his friends must have smuggled to him. But Matthias had on the sweater and pajama bottoms he'd worn the night he'd left Niedler School. He'd had them on under his Population Police uniform when he'd left headquarters. Some of his own blood had stained the sweater along with Percy's and Alia's.

"Want me to go in first?" Mike asked as they turned down a long driveway. "Just in case . . ."

Matthias knew he meant that the cottage full of friends might have been taken over by enemies. But Matthias shook his head.

"That's okay," he said. "I want to get this over with."

They walked up to the door together, even though it wasn't the wisest strategy. Matthias saw the glow in the windows, just like last time, and it made his heart ache even more. Last time he'd been so frantic, so filled with hope and fear. . . . This time he stood still and let Mike do the knocking.

Mr. Talbot opened the door.

"Nedley?" he whispered.

"The same," Mike replied, grinning. "Back from another wild ride."

The different name threw Matthias for a minute—was Mike's last name "Nedley"? And was he, too, a friend of Mr. Talbot's? But Matthias couldn't think about any of that right now. He couldn't even stop to say hello to Mr. Hendricks, rolling down the hall toward him. He had a mission.

He stepped forward.

"Mr. Talbot," Matthias said, "I came back to apologize to you. I'm sorry I took your wife into danger. I know you didn't want to let her go, and I'm sorry about what happened. It's my fault. I cared more about saving my friends than anything else. I've been at Population Police headquarters since—since she was killed, and all I could think about was losing Percy and Alia. They're gone now, and I can't apologize to them, but I can still tell you . . ."

He had so much more to say, but his voice trailed off because Mr. Talbot wasn't reacting right. Instead of bowing his head in sorrow, he reached out and buried Matthias in a great bear hug.

"Matthias! What a relief to see you! But why did you think Theodora was dead?" Mr. Talbot asked in amazement. He held Matthias out at arm's length so he could peer directly into his eyes. "She thought *you* were killed. She's right here. She and—"

Mr. Talbot gripped Matthias's shoulders and steered him toward the living room. Matthias's ears were ringing now, so loudly, he could barely hear Mr. Talbot's voice. He stumbled forward.

There, curled up on the couch before a cozy fire, was Mrs. Talbot, her red hair glowing. A boy and a girl sat on either side of her, looking healthy and happy, leaning over a book Mrs. Talbot had been reading with them. Only a faint scar still showed on the girl's forehead.

It was Percy and Alia.

MARGARET PETERSON HADDIX

CHAPTER FORTY-ONE

For a moment, all any of them could do was stare at each other, then Percy and Alia ran to Matthias and fell on him with hugs and shouts of joy.

"We thought you were dead!" Alia exclaimed, and Matthias shouted back, "I thought you were dead!" and somehow it was funny now, so they all had to laugh for a long time before anyone could explain.

"I saw you get into the car with the Population Police officer—was he taking you hostage?" Mrs. Talbot asked. "And then we heard a gunshot, and we just thought—"

"He shot a bird. Not me," Matthias said. "But he went back later and burned down everything for miles around the cabin, so I thought—"

"He did?" Mrs. Talbot asked. "Just recently, you mean?"

"No, that same day."

"No," Mrs. Talbot said, shaking her head firmly. "The cabin burned down, but that's all. And Percy and Alia and I were in the rebels' cave hideout, just up the hill from there, so we were safe. And then the rebels brought us back here, and we've been fine ever since."

Matthias stared at Mrs. Talbot in confusion. He still couldn't quite understand that she was real, that the friends he'd been mourning for months had been alive all along.

"But Tiddy said—," Matthias began. Then he remembered Tiddy telling the commander he'd been attacked by forty rebels, when there'd probably been only one. He remembered Tiddy claiming the Population Police hadn't killed the seventeen rebels at the cabin. "Oh," he breathed out. "Tiddy lied about the fire, too."

Why hadn't Matthias thought of that sooner? Why hadn't Matthias hung on to every last hope that his friends had survived?

It was being in Population Police headquarters, he thought. *It was so hard to believe in anything good there.*

And watching Tiddy die, right after he'd described the fire—that had seemed to confirm all Matthias's worst fears, made him believe the world was full of death and despair and there was no reason for hope.

And yet he'd escaped. And here were Percy and Alia, whole and healthy and grinning from ear to ear.

Matthias fell asleep that night in the same room as his friends. There were beds, but the three of them ended up huddled together on the floor, under cozy blankets, holding hands.

"I missed you so much," Alia murmured. "But we're together now."

"And we're safe here," Percy said.

"And the grown-ups will take care of us," Alia added.

"And God loves us," Percy finished.

Matthias woke the next morning long before the other two. In the dim winter light filtering in through the windows, he studied his friends' faces. Even in his sleep, Percy's expression was solemn. Matthias hoped he didn't still have nightmares about being shot.

Alia's face was harder to see because her hair covered her eyes. Matthias brushed back the golden strands and gently traced the scar on her forehead.

"My fault," he murmured.

Matthias slipped out from under the blankets and left the room. He found Mike and Mr. Talbot drinking coffee in the kitchen. He fixed himself a bowl of cereal and sat down with the grown-ups.

"Is your real name Nedley?" he asked Mike, because it was an easier question than all the others swirling around in his brain.

Mike threw his head back and laughed.

"It's the one I was using the last time I visited this cottage," Mike said. "But I've used lots of different names over the years. I'm not sure I even remember my real one."

"You were Nedley when you helped save my life," Mr. Talbot said. "You'll always be Nedley to me."

Matthias had the feeling Mike and Mr. Talbot could have told him a long story just then, but he already had enough to think about.

"I'm so happy that Percy and Alia—and Mrs. Talbot— are alive after all and that I found them again so they're not worrying about me," he began. "But why do I still feel . . ."

"Anxious?" Mr. Talbot offered.

"Troubled?" Mike said.

Matthias nodded, even though neither of those words exactly fit.

"It's not enough, is it?" he said. "Just to be with people you love, who love you. Not when there's so much evil in the world. I think it's like . . . God expects more of me."

He understood better now why Samuel had felt he had to go to the rally, why Mrs. Talbot had risked her life to rescue Percy and Alia. He was afraid that Mike and Mr. Talbot might make fun of him for mentioning God. But they were both gazing back at him with grave expressions.

"There's an old saying," Mr. Talbot said heavily. "'The only thing necessary for the triumph of evil is for good men to do nothing.' I've been thinking about that a lot myself lately. Because *I've* been doing nothing, these past few months."

"You were recovering from life-threatening injuries," Mike said.

"And now I'm recovered," Mr. Talbot said simply. "It's time to get back to work."

"Good," Mike said. "I'm glad to hear it."

The two of them shook hands as if they were making a solemn agreement. Matthias knew he'd just witnessed something important, but he was too caught up in his own dilemma to take much note of it.

"I never want to leave Percy and Alia again," he said. "If I go anywhere to fight the Population Police again, I'd want them to go with me."

Mr. Talbot frowned.

"They're little children, Matthias," he said quietly. "And they've already been through a lot."

Matthias wanted to ask, *What about me? Haven't I been through a lot? Aren't I a child too?* But the words died in his throat. He wasn't like Percy and Alia anymore. He'd crossed some line when he was apart from them. In the beginning, he'd been desperate to get back to them because he was lost without them; he didn't know who he was if he wasn't part of their cozy threesome. But now he knew just what Mr. Talbot meant. Percy and Alia were so young, so innocent—all he wanted to do was protect them.

"I'm thirteen," he choked out. "They're six and nine."

The ages were arbitrary numbers, little more than guesses. And claiming to be thirteen had been a stretch back in November when Tiddy had asked his age. But it sounded right now.

Mr. Talbot nodded solemnly.

"Yes," he said. "Thirteen is very different from six and nine."

"So then—," Mike said, as if expecting Matthias to announce eternal devotion to the cause now that he understood about Percy and Alia. Mike even had his hand half thrust out, as if he was ready to shake Matthias's hand too.

But Matthias was thinking about how hard it was to do anything good in a country run by the Population Police. He thought about how many times he'd messed up, hurting innocent children, endangering Percy and Alia, risking Nina's life when he protested her plan.

Oh, Samuel, he thought. *When you said to stay out of politics, you meant that it's easier to make sure you're doing good when you stay completely away from evil. You were a holy man. But even you had to go out into the world. You couldn't stand by when the Population Police were killing children.*

Then he thought about how even Mike, who was working for a good cause, had forgotten about the guard left behind in the warehouse and had kind of hoped that the commander would be killed.

Can I keep working with someone like that? Matthias thought. But he'd been the one who'd saved the guard. What if he hadn't been there?

Matthias sighed.

"I can't leave Percy and Alia now," he said. "Not when I just got here. But later on, if you need me . . ."

Mike nodded and clapped his hand on Matthias's shoulder.

"We'll need you," Mike said. "We'll need everyone who's capable of helping."

Matthias swallowed hard.

"Would I have to go back to Population Police headquarters?" he asked.

"I don't know," Mike said. "We need to figure out our next plan."

Matthias opened his mouth—then shut it again. He couldn't know exactly what he was signing on to. He couldn't know what choices he'd face, what agonizing options he'd have to decide between. But he knew he was doing the right thing.

Mr. Talbot put his hand on Matthias's other shoulder then and gave it a gentle squeeze. The three of them—Mike, Mr. Talbot, and Matthias—were linked in a little circle around the kitchen table, as if they were holding some sacred ceremony. But Matthias knew the circle of people working for good extended far beyond that kitchen table: to Nina, Trey, Lee and all the "others" she'd mentioned back at Population Police headquarters, to Mr. Hendricks and Mrs. Talbot elsewhere in the house, maybe even to Percy and Alia someday if the fight continued that long.

Matthias thought about what Mike had said most people would do if they'd been in Matthias's place at Population Police headquarters; he thought about the frightened people who'd taken their food back to the Population Police after the warehouse was destroyed. Most people, he realized, could see only the Population Police's power. But he knew the force for good was even stronger.

Even if I have to go back to Population Police headquarters, he thought, *even if I have to live among the enemy for years and years and years—even then, I will never be alone.*

He reached up and put one arm around Mike's shoulder and one arm around Mr. Talbot's, and that was like his part of the ceremony, his sacred pact.

We will keep fighting this evil, he was saying.

We will win.

Here's a look at Margaret Peterson Haddix's book *Found*, which launches her new series, The Missing.

Available now from
Simon & Schuster Books for Young Readers

It wasn't there. Then it was.

Later, that was how Angela DuPre would describe the airplane—over and over, to one investigator after another—until she was told never to speak of it again.

But when she first saw the plane that night, she wasn't thinking about mysteries or secrets. She was wondering how many mistakes she could make without getting fired, how many questions she dared ask before her supervisor, Monique, would explode, "That's it! You're too stupid to work at Sky Trails Air! Get out of here!" Angela had used a Post-it note to write down the code for standby passengers who'd received a seat assignment at the last minute, and she'd stuck it to her computer screen. She knew she had. But somehow, between the flight arriving from Saint Louis and the one leaving for Chicago, the Post-it had vanished. Any minute now, she thought, some standby passenger would show up at the counter asking for a boarding pass, and Angela would be forced to turn to Monique once more and mumble, "Uh, what was that code again?" And then Monique, who had perfect hair and perfect nails and a perfect tan and had probably been born knowing all the Sky Trails codes, would grit her teeth and narrow her eyes and repeat the code in that slow fake-patient voice she'd been using with Angela all night, the voice that said behind the words, *I know you're severely mentally challenged, so I will try not to speak faster than one word per minute, but you have to realize, this is a real strain for me because I am so vastly superior. . . .*

Angela was not severely mentally challenged. She'd done fine in school and at the Sky Trails orientation. It was just, this was her first actual day on the job, and Monique had been nasty from the very start. Every one of Monique's frowns and glares and insinuations kept making Angela feel more panicky and stupid.

Sighing, Angela glanced up. She needed a break from staring at the computer screen longing for a lost Post-it. She peered out at the passengers crowding the terminal: tired-looking families sprawled in seats, dark-suited businessmen sprinting down the aisle. Which one of them would be the standby flier who'd rush up to the counter and ruin Angela's life? Generally speaking, Angela had always liked people; she wasn't used to seeing them as threats. She forced her gaze beyond the clumps of passengers, to the huge plate glass window on the other side of the aisle. It was getting dark out, and Angela could see the runway lights twinkling in the distance.

Runway, runaway, she thought vaguely. And then—had she blinked?—suddenly the lights were gone. No, she corrected herself, *blocked.* Suddenly there was an airplane between Angela and the runway lights, an airplane rolling rapidly toward the terminal.

Angela gasped.

"What now?" Monique snarled, her voice thick with exasperation.

"That plane," Angela said. "At gate 2B. I thought it—" What was she supposed to say? *Wasn't there? Appeared out of thin air?*—I thought it was going too fast and might run into the building," she finished in a rush, because suddenly that had seemed true too. She watched as the plane pulled to a stop, neatly aligned with the jetway. "But it . . . didn't. No worries."

Monique whirled on Angela.

"Never," she began, in a hushed voice full of suppressed rage, "never, ever, ever say anything like that. Weren't you paying attention in orientation? Never say you think a plane is going to crash. Never say a plane could crash. Never even use the word *crash*. Do you understand?"

"Okay," Angela whispered. "Sorry."

But some small rebellious part of her brain was thinking, *I didn't use the word* crash. *Weren't you paying attention to me? And if a plane really was going to run into the building, wouldn't Sky Trails want its employees to warn people, to get them out of the way?*

Just as rebelliously, Angela kept watching the plane parked at 2B, instead of bending her head back down to concentrate on her computer.

"Um, Monique?" she said after a few moments. "Should one of us go over there and help the passengers unload—er, I mean—deplane?" She was proud of herself for remembering to use the official airline-sanctioned word for unloading.

Beside her, Monique rolled her eyes.

"The gate agents responsible for 2B," she said in a tight voice, "will handle deplaning there."

Angela glanced at the 2B counter, which was silent and dark and completely unattended. There wasn't even a message scrolling across the LCD sign behind the counter to indicate that the plane had arrived or where it'd come from.

"Nobody's there," Angela said stubbornly.

Frowning, Monique finally glanced up.

"Great. Just great," she muttered. "I always have to fix everyone else's mistakes." She began stabbing her perfectly manicured nails at her computer keyboard. Then she stopped, mid-stab. "Wait—that can't be right."

"What is it?" Angela asked.

Monique was shaking her head.

"Must be pilot error," she said, grimacing in disgust. "Some yahoo pulled up to the wrong gate. There's not supposed to be anyone at that gate until the Cleveland flight at nine thirty."

Angela considered telling Monique that if Sky Trails had banned *crash* from their employees' vocabulary, that maybe passengers should be protected from hearing *pilot error* as well. But Monique was already grabbing the telephone, barking out orders.

"Yeah, Bob, major screwup," she was saying. "You've got to get someone over here. . . . No, I don't know which gate it was supposed to go to. How would I know? Do you think I'm clairvoyant? . . . No, I can't see the numbers on the plane. Don't you know it's dark out?"

With her free hand, Monique was gesturing frantically at Angela.

"At least go open the door!" she hissed.

"You mean . . ."

"The door to the jetway!" Monique said, pointing. Angela hoped that some of the contempt on Monique's face was intended for Bob, not just her. Angela imagined meeting Bob someday, sharing a laugh at Monique's expense. Still, dutifully, she walked over to the 2B waiting area and pulled open the door to the hallway that led down to the plane.

Nobody came out.

Angela picked a piece of lint off her blue skirt and then stood at attention, her back perfectly straight, just like in the training videos. Maybe she couldn't keep track of standby codes, but she was capable of standing up straight.

Still, nobody appeared.

Angela began to feel foolish, standing so alertly by an open door that no one was using. She bent her head and peeked down the jetway—it was deserted and turned at such an angle that she couldn't see all the way down to the plane, to see if anyone had opened the door to the jet yet. She backed up a little and peered out the window, straight down to the cockpit of the plane. The cockpit was dark, its windows blank, and that struck Angela as odd. She'd been on the job for only five hours, and she'd been a little distracted. But she was pretty sure that when planes landed, the pilots stayed in the cockpit for a while filling out paperwork or something. She thought that they at least waited until all the passengers were off before they turned out the cockpit lights.

Angela peeked down the empty jetway once more and went back to Monique.

"Of course I'm sure there's a plane at that gate! I can see it with my own eyes!" Monique was practically screaming into the phone. She shook her head at Angela, and for the first time it was almost in a companionable way, as if to say, *At least you know there's a plane there! Unlike the other morons I have to deal with!* Monique cupped her hand over the receiver and fumed to Angela, "The incompetence around here is unbelievable! The control tower says that plane never landed, never showed up on the radar. The Sky Trails dispatcher says we're not missing a plane—everything that was supposed to land in the past hour pulled up to the right gate, and all the other planes due to arrive within the next hour or so are accounted for. How could so many people just lose a plane?"

Or, how could we find it? Angela thought. The whole situation was beginning to seem strange to her, otherworldly. But maybe that was just a function of being new to the job, of having spent so much time concentrating on the computer and being yelled at by Monique. Maybe airports lost and found planes all the time, and that was just one of those things nobody had mentioned in the Sky Trails orientation.

"Did, uh, anybody try to contact the pilot?" Angela asked cautiously.

"Of course!" Monique said. "But there's no answer. He must be on the wrong frequency."

Angela thought of the dark cockpit, the way she hadn't been able to see through the windows. She decided not to mention this.

"Should I go back and wait? . . ."

Monique nodded fiercely and went back to yelling into the phone: "What do you mean, this isn't your responsibility? It's not my responsibility either!"

Angela was glad to put a wide aisle and two waiting areas between herself and Monique again. She went back to the jetway door by gate 2B. The sloped hallway leading down to the plane was still empty, and the colorful travel posters lining the walls—"Sky Trails! Your ticket to the world!"—seemed jarringly bright. Angela stepped into the jetway.

I'll just go down far enough to see if the jet door is open, she told herself. *It may be a violation of protocol, but Monique won't notice, not when she's busy yelling at everyone else in the airport. . . .*

At the bend in the ramp, Angela looked around the corner. She had a limited view, but caught a quick glimpse of a flight attendants' little galley, with neatly stowed drink carts. Obviously, the jet door was standing wide open. She started to turn around, already beginning to debate with herself about whether she should report this information to Monique. Then she heard—what? A whimper? A cry?

Angela couldn't exactly identify the sound, but it was enough to pull her on down the jetway.

New Sky Trails employee saves passenger on first day on job, she thought to herself, imagining the praise and congratulations—and maybe the raise—she'd be sure to receive if what she was visualizing was real. She'd learned CPR in the orientation session. She knew basic first aid. She knew where every emergency phone in the airport was located. She started walking faster, then running.

On the side of the jet, she was surprised to see a strange insignia: TACHYON TRAVEL, it said, some airline Angela had never heard of. Was that a private charter company maybe? And then, while she was staring at it, the words suddenly changed into the familiar wing-in-the-clouds symbol of Sky Trails.

Angela blinked.

That couldn't have happened, she told herself. *It was just an optical illusion, just because I was running, just because I'm worried about whoever made that cry or whimper. . . .*

Angela stepped onto the plane. She turned her head

first to the left, looking into the cockpit. Its door also stood open, but the small space was empty, the instruments dark.

"Hello?" Angela called, looking to the right now, expecting to see some flight attendant with perfectly applied makeup—or maybe some flight attendant and a pilot bent over a prone passenger, maybe an old man suddenly struck down by a heart attack or a stroke. Or, at the very least, passengers crowding the aisle, clutching laptops and stuffed animals brought from faraway grandparents' homes, overtired toddlers crying, fragile old women calling out to taller men, "Could you pull my luggage down from the overhead for me? It's that red suitcase over there. . . ."

But the aisle of this airplane was as empty and silent as its cockpit. Angela could see all the way to the back of the plane, and not a single person stood in her view, not a single voice answered her.

Only then did Angela drop her gaze to the passenger seats. They stretched back twelve rows, with two seats per row on the left side of the aisle and one each on the right. She stepped forward, peering at all of them. Thirty-six seats on this plane, and every single one of them was full.

Each seat contained a baby.

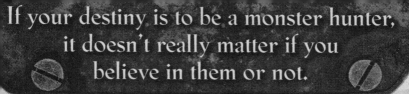

If your destiny is to be a monster hunter, it doesn't really matter if you believe in them or not.

The first book in
THE HUNTER CHRONICLES
series is in stores fall 2011.

The Hunter Chronicles
Snare #1: Return to Exile

THE SEARCH

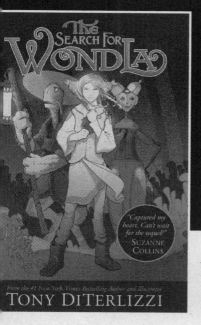

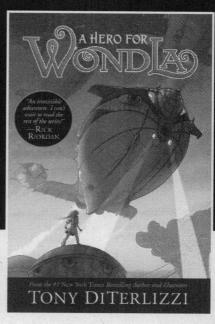

is just the beginning....